I0785173

Tomorrow Can Worry About Itself

A Strangely Unfamiliar Novel

By

Dawn Evans

New Gal Publishing
Photograph on cover by Svengine,
"Watch movement," Getty Images via Canva

Made in the USA
2023

Library of Congress
ISBN #: 979-8-9867096-1-1

Acknowledgements

To the Lord God Almighty, my Father in heaven who has given me life, purpose, a future and a hope. And the faith that I can do all things He has called me to do.

To my dad here on earth who has always encouraged me in that life, purpose, future and hope. Who raised me to love being who God made me, while never making me feel like a burden to him.

To Dava, my sister in the faith, who kicked me in the pants from time to time to live that life, purpose, future and hope. And who never looked at me crazy for having a dream.

A special thanks to the New Gal Publishing Team, Cyndi and Dyanna, you're the best.

"Because, although they knew God, they did not glorify Him as God, nor were thankful, but became futile in their thoughts, and their foolish hearts were darkened. Professing to be wise, they became fools, and changed the glory of the incorruptible God into an image made like corruptible man…" Romans 1:21–23

CHAPTER ONE

Who decorates an entire train station lobby with clocks? And not even the same clocks, but different shapes, sizes and colors, even the time read on each face was different. Each clock was a second ahead of the one to the left of it as they were arranged across the walls of the station lobby. Their only commonality was that every clock was analog. It was a pretentious attempt at art when it was obvious that this was in fact a time subway station. Actually, this was the first year of the first time-traveling subway station. So the clocks were a bit much. But that was how the Time Consortium overdid everything. Even time travel itself. The first time mechanism was created a few years before I was born. I don't know the specifics of it and there were so many rumors and conspiracy theories surrounding its birth or discovery that I didn't bother to invest study in its history. All I know is that at some point after the restructuring taught the world that natural order could be broken, people no longer saw a use for the Creator or any other higher power to direct their lives. With time travel, one could simply see the outcome of any decision and, if things went wrong the decision could be undone. Of course what seems simple in theory almost never is in action. Somewhere after the creation of the mechanism the world powers established The Consortium of Time Travel, a way of regulating time travel to the subway station alone, for a profit to each participating country. Of course plenty of private individuals attempted constructing their own means of time travel, which never seemed to pan out safely. So the Consortium Station was the best and most logical choice for a vacation ten years in the past or sight-seeing forty years in the future. I wasn't here now for either of those things. Actually I was on my way home, whenever that was? I'd just been paroled from the Preservation after a ten-year sentence. With new innovations paving a way, illegal activity isn't far behind. So not long after establishing the station for time travel, the Consortium established its own prison for time crimes and called it, The Preservation. The name may sound like a sweet retreat or white-collar lockup, but in reality, it has a much more sinister background.

Critiquing the clocks had no real purpose in my trip home, other than a means of wasting time, and maybe a little bit of nostalgia. A normal parolee wasn't allowed to time travel again for at least two years or more, depending on time served. But I was no normal parolee and, at eighty-six years old, this trip home would be the last jump through time I would ever make. I was barred from travel for the rest of my life, however much longer that turned out to be. I chew my bottom lip and study each clock face thoroughly. Time always fascinated me and scared me. I couldn't get enough of it when I wanted more and couldn't give it away when I had too much. God's practical joke on me I guess? Which is why I didn't mind taking time into my own hands ... or at least into the hands of the world powers. And yet, I was still undecided on whose authority I could do better under. I tap the thick paper of my Preservation issued ticket against my open palm and try to work up the nerve to catch my train.

"Are you looking for your clock?" Startled, I look for the source of the question. There is a small child standing right beside me. I hadn't even noticed her. I force my best old lady smile and hope security doesn't notice the two of us together. The poor thing doesn't know about fines and tickets yet. But she will.

"I was looking for my clock, but I can't seem to find it," I reply. The little girl is holding a man's watch in her hands. A much younger version of the one on my wrist. It was oversized then and still slightly so now. I had to make extra holes for the band to fit. I quickly examine the lobby for her dad as the little girl plays with his watch. He was probably at the front desk trying to find out why her mom's train hadn't arrived yet. According to the station, the trains were never late, until today I suppose. Although neither of us knew at the time that it wasn't late at all. It had arrived already but was held up by security downstairs on the platform. My dad always gave me his watch when we were at the station and sent me off to this hideous display to find the one clock that was accurate to his own, down to the second. I point to the watch in the kid's hand.

"Are you looking for your clock, too?" She smiles back. It was a good way to keep me occupied and make sure I didn't wander off.

"Have you ever found your clock before?" I ask.

"No, the seconds move too fast," she replies.

"Yeah, time will do that." The little girl touches the watch on my arm gently, pushing the band up to see the dark mark around my wrist underneath.

"Were you in the Preservation?" she asks. I pull my hand away before she makes real contact with my skin. I can just barely feel the electrical pulse of her fingertips and it makes the hairs on my arm stand up. I hate the cross-line shock and try to avoid it as much as I avoid other versions of myself. It only happens when a person comes in physical contact with themselves from another time period or timeline. Normally I don't even cross paths with myself in the station. There was one time but...I won't talk about that one time.

"How do you know about the Preservation?" I ask playfully. How did I know about the Preservation back then? The little girl shrugs.

"At school I heard all the prisoners there have to repeat the worst days of their lives over and over again until they go crazy." She was close, but not quite.

"You should get back to your father. Your mommy will be here soon." I hated to lie to the kid, but what else could I say? The little girl stares curiously at my watch and then her own. If she notices, she's not saying anything.

"Did you break out of the Preservation?" Her eyes are wide with excitement at the idea of talking to an escaped criminal.

"No one breaks out of the Preservation. I was released and now I'm going home." The girl becomes somber again, probably disappointed that I was released legally. She points at my watch again.

"Is that mark from the bracelet?" I nod. Every prisoner has to wear a time loop band on their wrist which leaves a dark mark like a regrettable tattoo. A reminder of my bondage. Obviously covering it with the watch didn't do much good. Before I can say anymore, the little girl's father appears and calls out her unusual name.

"Yes, Daddy?" the girl replies. Her father motions for her

to follow him and leave the nice old lady alone. The little girl complies and waves goodbye. I wave back and watch father and daughter together for a moment. Sometimes the station has its purpose for replaying memories like these. The old way of memories under The Creator was too bittersweet for me? But to be honest, either way it still hurts somehow. Because to see, even now, is to be reminded that beautiful moments like these, usually come to an ugly end. I turn away and shove my ticket in my pocket. I grab the paper bag with my belongings off the plastic chair and head for the check-in desk. I take one last look at my father and my six-year-old self and smile. In that moment, at six years old, I had committed my first time violation by talking to myself and I hadn't even known it. My criminal career started much younger than I thought.

CHAPTER TWO

In the first year of the first time travel station there were seven check-in departments for travel. One for each continent recognized on the globe at the time. Each department had only five check-in desks, representing each participating country. It was necessary to verify a person's identity, natural timeline, country of origin, last known addresses, whether the traveler was still alive in the timeline in which they were traveling, and where they were living in that timeline so there would be no illegal meetings with a traveler's past or future self, all before an individual could make a jump. So time travel passports came into existence to track an individual and make travel less stressing or complicated. But no one really believed that. The truth was that since there were time travel criminals, there must be time travel crimes, and you can't have time travel crimes without time travel laws. The list of laws is longer than I care to go over, but they do include things like meeting yourself in another time period outside of a sanctioned meeting in the station. Most people ignored this law because the punishment was usually no more than a ticket with a hefty fine—a ridiculously high amount, which people were willing to pay; if it meant catching up on all the latest information with your former or future self. Some believed it could save them the heartbreak of a costly mistake but, in my experience, knowing doesn't do you any good to change things for the better. Some people attempted to gain odds on gambling, but time travelers were banned from casinos and any wins made weren't released until it was verified that the player hadn't met with their future self to get insider information. The same with lottery winners and any other game of chance where time travel could be exploited to gain an advantage.

Each violation could result in something much worse than a ticket. Like time in the Preservation. Since it was also illegal to travel the subway systems without a Consortium-issued time passport, the punishment for which could get a person five to ten years, I opted out of searching for one on the black market, even though it would be faster, and figured it better to just get in line and get my paperwork legit so I could go home. I chose a line by size, and that proved to be a mistake since there were only six people in front of me, but the person at the desk was the mother of a family just returning from eighty years in the future, only to realize the family dog had been left behind, or forward (you know what I mean). As I stood in line, I took the watch off and placed it in my pocket. The sweat collecting under it was making the mark on my wrist itch.

"Watch out! Watch out!" Two lines over, a man's luggage cart falls to the floor, scattering all his bags across the lobby tile. Followed by the sound of children laughing. I could just make out the faint image of two phantom children circling the fallen bags, giggling hysterically.

"I hate those little brats," says the woman behind me. Her companion steps out of the line to help the gentleman with his luggage. Two associates also come over to help with the cleanup as the phantom children fade out again and all that remains of them is their laughter echoing across the lobby towards the escalators. Their giggles eventually faded into the darkness of the subway platform below. The woman behind me points to the spilled luggage while looking at me.

"And if you ask me, that woman should rot in the Preservation for the rest of her life." I didn't have it in me to tell her we didn't know each other and to point out that she and I weren't initially in a conversation, so I just nod politely at her complaints. 'That woman' she was referring to was Cathy Morgan. Cathy was serving a ninety-nine year sentence in the Preservation for killing her sister, Geenie, repeatedly throughout time. As Cathy claimed at the private hearing, she didn't want to share the inheritance of her family's estate with Geenie, so Cathy used the subway systems to go back in time two years prior to the will reading to dispose of her sister. The only problem was that upon her return Cathy discovered with the altered timeline that her parents placed all their money in establishing a college fund in Geenie's name to give her some kind of legacy before their own deaths, leaving Cathy with less to inherit than she started with. Cathy then went back even further to kill Geenie at an earlier time, hoping that her parents wouldn't come up with the same idea. They didn't. When Cathy returned her parents had burned through their finances trying to mourn. So once again Cathy got less than what she would've gotten had she just left things alone. After six trips back in time to kill her sister, Cathy could come out no better. Her final trip was when her mother was pregnant with Geenie. Cathy's idea was to make her mother miscarry and incidentally Cathy's mother died as well from some kind of complications a year later. Leaving Cathy's father to remarry another woman and have six more children in which Cathy would have to share her inheritance. By the time Cathy had given up she had done so much damage murdering her sister repeatedly that she caused a sort of fracture in Geenie's timeline. She didn't just change the past––she broke it, so to speak. And, to make matters worse, it also caused the first phantoms that anyone knew of. Every trip anyone took to the past was supposed to be monitored specifically so nothing could be changed in the future. The problem was too many people traveling and not nearly enough ways to monitor them all, at all times. So some changes made it through the cracks, and anytime something was changed it caused remnants of what could've been. Sometimes those remnants were memories of things you've never done but can specifically remember doing. Other times there were people who knew you but you couldn't place them or vice versa. Items appearing in your home or on your person that you never bought or owned; suddenly manifesting themselves and sometimes disappearing again just as mysteriously. These were usually small or inconsequential things. But the phantoms were something deeper, something bigger. I'd only seen them a few times in the station. Mostly little children running around and pulling pranks. The occasional teenager moping in a plastic chair and even a few adults riding the trains until they made a jump through the time mechanism, then the train would come out the other side with an empty seat. All the phantoms in the station were suspected to be Geenie's 'would've been' children. The children she had, but didn't have, because her life was altered so drastically with multiple deaths working in reverse all the way back to her own birth. The phantoms were lives that never got the chance to live but at one point were meant to come into being and did. Always on the brink of existence, but not existing. I don't think I'd ever seen a phantom outside of the station, but who knew? Now they just caused havoc through the stations, the trains and occasionally the lobby.

With the man's bags settled back on his cart, a station agent takes him to another booth, most likely to expedite his paperwork and get him on his way as an apology for the disturbance. The companion of the woman behind me, who I assume is her husband, returns to his wife who catches him up on our one-sided conversation about Cathy Morgan.

"Ted, I was just telling this lady here about how that Cathy woman got off easy with all the trouble she caused." I try to pull away from the discussion but the woman keeps motioning her husband to look at me as if she doesn't want me to leave. Ted rolls his eyes and it's obvious they've been on this topic before and he's tired of it.

"Helen, let it go. I think ninety-nine years is more than enough time for a mistake." Ted replies. Helen's eyes widen in offense.

"More than enough time? And what mistake? What she did wasn't a mistake."

"I'm not condoning attempted murder..."

"There was no attempt. She didn't try, she did. She murdered someone, repeatedly. That's just as bad as a serial killer. And what about her mother? You do remember she managed to kill her own mother as well. I don't even think the high court held her responsible for that one. They couldn't have and only given her ninety-nine years!"

"Helen, relax. It's over and she's not getting out alive. Once the ninety-years are up she'll be executed."

"I don't mean to get riled up about it, but I just don't understand how a person could do something like that? And no one takes into account her creating the phantoms. She killed them too, technically. Now because of her they can't exist, but they do exist, and the whole thing makes no sense." Helen is addressing me again now, and I smile politely but say nothing. Best to just let this conversation die out on its own. Considering what she'd done and why, I had a feeling Cathy enjoyed when people talked about her. Maybe the infamy made up for her loss of freedom.

"And on top of all that you stand there and say that it's more than enough time for a mistake?" Ted shrugs. Well, when you put it that way...

"Well, maybe I misspoke? But if ninety-nine years is being lenient, then the fact that she won't die before then and is condemned to serve every last year of that sentence should suffice." Helen crosses her arms over her chest and frowns while checking out the front of the line.

"If you say so. Of course she won't die of natural causes or old age, but she could commit suicide." A harsh suggestion, but it was likely. The format of the Preservation was more psychological punishment than physical threat. Living the same day over and over for a lifetime could force a person to take drastic measures to end a life the prison was forcing them to live. It was the reason for the time loop bands. The first day of a prisoner's sentence was on repeat every day for the rest of their sentence. It's why no one ever aged in the Preservation. We were stuck in a twenty-two hour loop. Our only break was the two-hour work detail of assembling replacement parts for the time mechanisms used in the station. The line finally began to move, and I assume they had figured something out with the time-wandering pooch. As I took a few steps forward I felt something sharp digging into my leg, just over my ankle. I wince and look down. There was nothing on the floor. I crouch down and lift the hem of my jeans to find two cuts just above my ankle bone. They sting and I search my pockets for a tissue or something to clean up the blood. Helen notices.

"Are you okay?"

"Yes, I think so. I must've cut myself on something this morning and didn't even notice." Helen retrieves a napkin from her purse and I thank her as I dab at the blood. I wrap the napkin around my ankle and pull my sock up to hold it in place before standing up again.

"So strange. I didn't even feel it until now." I explain to Helen.

"So where are you traveling to?" She asks.

"I'm going home actually. I've been out here for the last ten years. My original time now is in the eightieth year station, I believe." Helen looks surprised and nudges her husband.

"See Ted, it's good to travel as we get older. She's still getting around and seeing the world,' Helen speaks to me. "Ted hates time traveling. I love it. We can see family and friends long gone..."

"I didn't say I hated it. I just said I'd rather do time the way it's supposed to be done. All this jumping around makes a person forget where they really belong," Ted explains. "And not everyone who has died is someone I want to see again," Ted mumbles.

"I hope you're not referring to my mother!" Helen snaps. Ted says nothing and I interject.

"You're right about time being confusing. I'm not sure where I belong now either," I reply. Helen frowns.

"Well, I still love it. But to be honest the only thing I'm not really a fan of is the waiting in line...and the paperwork...and the phantoms...oh, and I can't stand all the criminals that come through here. It seems like every day there is another criminal transport coming in. It's very dangerous. They shouldn't be allowed around the public." I rub my wrist self-consciously and Ted notices. Slightly alarmed, Ted tries to quiet his wife.

"Okay, Helen, we get it."

"I'm not trying to complain. I'm just saying it makes me uncomfortable. I'll never understand why this first year station is more like a crime court." It was true. The Preservation was located just down the road from here, but the prison registry for time criminals was housed in the first year station alone. Meaning every new convict was brought to the first year station to be processed and admitted to the prison. The first year station is also where everyone had to go to pay fines, tickets and attend time crime court on the fourth floor. Which I was all too familiar with.

"And what I really don't understand is why there are time criminals in the first place. Wouldn't it make more sense to just go back in time before someone commits the crime and stop them?" I open my mouth to respond but Ted beats me to it.

"They can't do that anymore, Helen. You know it's illegal now."

"But that's what's so stupid! Why is it illegal? It's the one thing that could've stopped Cathy Morgan from doing what she did."

"It's because of the lawsuits." Helen and Ted look at me in surprise.

"What lawsuits?" Helen asks.

"Well, I'm not sure which year they started in, but in the first few years of the station the justice department did use time travel to arrest people for future crimes. Then one year a college student named Ruby Tammer got arrested for killing her husband about twenty years in her future. Ruby hadn't even met her future husband yet. Actually at the time of her arrest he was just a classmate she never really noticed. Ruby argued the charge and claimed that she didn't have it in her to kill anyone but the facts didn't lie. She had killed him. Shot him point blank when she found out he was stealing money from their joint account and was planning to leave her. Anyway, Ruby was granted a trial to plead her case, and in the middle of the trial her future husband was hit by a car and died anyway. It threw the whole case into a tailspin. Could the court charge Ruby for a crime she couldn't possibly commit now? Agents went forward in time and couldn't find anything to hold Ruby on. Not even a parking ticket. She did get married to another man though and they stayed together for almost sixty years, until Ruby's death. They had to let her go and Ruby sued the Consortium for having her arrested in the first place. Every action in the present causes a reaction in the future. Timelines are consistently changing based off of our choices and the Justice Department realized that if they arrested everyone for a crime they might commit in the future, the arrest alone could change the future to where no crime was committed. And if no crime was committed, the argument was that no one should've been arrested. So a law was made that no one could be arrested for a future crime and no evidence could be acquired through time travel or admitted into a case." Ted begins to laugh and Helen grows angry.

"Unbelievable. I've never heard of anything so ridiculous," Helen snaps.

"I remember that story now. I read a few bits about the trial when we were on vacation in the future but I never knew all that. Did Ruby win her lawsuit?" Ted asks.

"She did. She won a pretty hefty sum, I believe..."

"And I'm sure we're all paying for it now with the hike in ticket prices," Helen adds. She was right.

"Wait. Why didn't the Consortium just go back in time and not arrest Ruby? Then they wouldn't get sued. Oh, but then the young man would get killed by Ruby anyway right?" Ted continues trying to answer his own question. Helen rolls her eyes.

"Give me a break. The Consortium doesn't care about that

man or his life. I'm sure they would let him die if they could get their money back," Helen explains.

"From what I remember, Ruby refused to allow the Consortium to change her past and if they'd done it anyway there would've been some remnant of the change, possibly even a phantom or two, and most likely without the law that's in place now against arrests before the crime, Ruby could've and would've just sued them after she killed her husband on the grounds that the Consortium didn't stop her from committing murder when they could have," I explain.

"You see, this is what I mean about time travel. That part I don't like. The idiocy of the laws and rules. And they're not stopping a single crime! But all of us law-abiding citizens get held up in a line for hours just to visit my mother for the week. It's ridiculous!" I'm next at the desk finally and I make my escape from the conversation.

CHAPTER THREE

"Hi, I'm here to get my travel paperwork." I hand my identification and my issued ticket across the counter to the very pregnant clerk.

"I'm sorry my identification is expired in my own time. It was still valid when I was arrested though." I don't know why I'm trying to explain? Just nervous about going home, I suppose. The clerk shrugs and begins typing on her computer.

"It's alright. Technically it wasn't even issued yet. You're only what…' The clerk leans in close to read my license. "Six years old in this year. The ID is only a formality to prove you are who you are."

"If I was anyone else I certainly wouldn't pick this identity to hide in." The clerk laughs at my bitter joke and I lean on the counter just waiting.

"Is that your real name? I thought it was a misprint on your ticket. That is adorable." I nod in appreciation of the compliment. I never favored my name or the ridiculous story of how I got it. In my opinion it never paired well with my identity.

"Is it pronounced El-See?" The clerk asks.

"No, it's just Else. Like anything else or something else or, or else. Just Else."

"I think I might have to steal that one." The clerk responds as she rubs her belly. I look away and try to pretend it doesn't bother me.

"Miss Ramses, do you happen to have a paper copy of your release form? I'm not able to locate one for you in the system." I blink not really understanding the question.

"I'm sorry, what?" The clerk repeats herself and I search my paper bag. Nothing but the few items I'd been arrested with. I reach deeper into the bag and my fingers touch the packet of seeds at the bottom. I pull my hand out of the bag as if I'd been bitten and shake my head.

"No, I don't have anything else. I wasn't given anything." Was I? I don't remember being given any paperwork. The clerk frowns and attempts to find my papers in the system again.

"Okay, it seems I can't locate any information on you. I have no release papers for you. But no worries, it could be a delay on the part of the Preservation. To be honest I've never handled a parolee traveling, but I'm sure we can figure this out." My heart is beating faster now.

"So, what should I do? I don't want to miss my train." The clerk takes a book out of her desk and begins to look something up. She smiles as she seems to find what she is looking for and I get my hopes up.

"Okay, I found it." The clerk begins typing again and the printer begins to spit out some pages. The clerk takes the stack of pages and slides them across the desk to me.

"Okay, now I just need you to fill these out and take the finished copies upstairs to the third floor of the sixth year station. Also…" The clerk fills out a portal pass and hands it to me. "Upon your return to this station, go to the fourth floor to see the Secretary of Preservation Affairs and they will get you all situated." So much for hope.

"But what about my train? What if I miss it?" The clerk's smile doesn't waver.

"There will always be another train." The clerk hands an ink pen to me and I walk away from the desk, overwhelmed by what just happened.

"Did she just say Preservation Affairs?' I can hear Helen fussing at Ted as I walk away. "You mean to tell me that sweet looking little old lady is a criminal? And I was talking to her this whole time."

"Helen, calm down!" Ted snaps. I clutch the papers to my chest and head for the elevators.

CHAPTER FOUR

On the ride up to the third floor I begin playing with the ink pen from the clerk which reads, "Time waits for no one" printed across the cheap plastic body. The Consortium's motto, sort of. I hold the papers out in front of me and flip through the pages I'm supposed to fill out. This is ridiculous. I just want to go home. I try not to show my frustration in front of the other two people in the elevator. Once on the third floor, just as I'm stepping out behind the couple my papers fly out of my hand and into the air. I feel little fingers pinching my arms and I take blind swings at the phantom children as they laugh and circle me. I hiss at one little boy to my right that is solidifying in front of me wearing a pair of swimming trunks. I'd heard that some phantoms could change, age in front of people, but this was the first time I'd ever seen it for myself. The boy went from about six or seven to around twelve or thirteen in just a few seconds. His swimming trunks and wet hair changing with him to a baseball uniform and a neat haircut. Then he reached his teens in jeans and a shirt, his hair dyed black and hanging over his eyes. By his twenties his head was shaved and his uniform became fatigues. Then, just like that, he vanishes and I'm alone in the hallway. What a strange encounter. Embarrassed I kneel down and begin to gather all the papers back together. The sheets are all in disarray and I sit on a nearby bench trying to put them back in order. As I'm shuffling the papers I realize that this is an application for a travel passport. Why would I have to fill that out if I already have one? I only need one pass to get me back home, and then I never have to come back to this stupid station again. I slam the papers on the bench in frustration and stare at the portal box at the end of the hall. The portal boxes are like elevators that go neither up or down, but forward and backward in the timeline of the station. Being inside of a portal is much like being in an elevator with that feeling as your stomach drops when it lifts up or down. Except in a portal it's about fifty times stronger and it's more like your insides have been shot into another time period and your skin has to catch up.

Every portal in the station was constructed with a connection to the single secondary, smaller version of the time mechanism, which powers it to allow one person at a time to travel from one year of the station to another. While the trains could take a person practically all over the world at any time in the world at their leisure, by using a much larger time mechanism, the portals were originally reserved for Consortium and station business. This meant you didn't need a passport or identification to travel in one and, most importantly you didn't have to pay. The only two downsides were that while traveling through time portals the individual still couldn't leave the station without the proper paperwork. And a parolee banned from travel couldn't use the portals either. Without a pass, of course. Even though the portals were originally constructed for station employees and officials to maneuver through time for Consortium-related business, travelers found ways to sneak on, and the free-and-quick jump had become so popular among school children and the eternally bored, that the Consortium opened the portals on each floor for the use of the patrons. I hated jumping through the portal. It was nauseating and uncomfortable. But right now it was the only way I was going to get home. Well, that and filling out this ridiculous paperwork. Might as well get it done now. I start the first page with my name and age. But I get stuck at the current address. I'm not sure if my prison residency counts, but I quickly write in the Preservation anyway and move to the next question. My last known address before my current address? My parent's old house. I close my eyes trying to remember the street number? Fifty-eight twenty-three or twenty-three fifty-eight? I'd grown up in that house and only moved out to go to school and when I got married, and now I couldn't even remember the address! In frustration I give up and move on to the next question. And of course they went on like this for the next seven questions. Only some kind of robot could remember all their previous addresses going back through nine different locations? Once I moved I could care less where I used to live; I didn't live there anymore. Okay, next page. Employment? That's not happening. My last job before my arrest was a factory that I'm sure has long since gone out of business. My very first job as a teen was cleaning offices in one of the future stations, possibly the tenth or eleventh year station? Of course that wasn't so much a job as I think it was a community service, because I don't remember getting paid. I set the papers down knowing if I try to fill out any more I was going to scream. I give up and shove the papers and the pen in my paper bag and head for the portal. Might as well jump now, while I still have the nerve.

CHAPTER FIVE

According to the clerk I would have to travel to the sixth year of the station to turn the paperwork in and get it processed. After that I'd have to come back to the first year and go to the fourth floor for my meeting. This was ridiculous. I would just have to explain to them where I've been and what I'm trying to do and that I don't need a passport. After this trip home I wasn't doing any more time traveling, so I had no more use for a passport. I had no more use for this station and I was glad to be away from it. I felt like all the worse moments of my life took place here in one time or another. As I approach the portal box I notice there is no line but a single attendant standing in front of the doors staring at the safety light overhead. Every portal box had a red light above the doors to signal to the attendant whether or not the path was clear to send someone through. According to some old myth, if one person jumped through a portal heading for a time period and someone else jumped through another portal leaving the time period the first person was coming to, the two could cross paths and sort of…merge. I didn't want to imagine what that looked like.

"You're not heading for the box, are you?" I stop a few feet from the portal and turn around. There is a line of about a dozen people all leaning against the wall or sitting on the nearby bench looking irritated.

"I was." I reply to the man in the front of the line who is addressing me. The man nods to the portal.

"They've got a prison transport coming in. This is the line when they're done. We have to wait here where it's safe. Apparently they have an extremely dangerous individual coming in." Before I can ask another question the elevator opens up, revealing six armed guards. I stand in the center of the aisle watching the guards as they march past me and approach the box. The attendant hands his portal key to a single guard and disappears into a small room behind the attendant desk. With no one but the guards in front of the box, the guard inserts the key into a control panel on the wall and waits. As soon as the light turns red the guard turns the key and stands back along with the rest of his team. A light comes on overhead inside the box and gets brighter and brighter until it is a blinding burst which fills the box then everything in the box goes dark and an ice like film appears across the glass doors. With their weapons drawn, as the film begins to clear, the first guard opens the door to the portal and there is a small young man inside with his arms stretched up over his head as his wrists are chained to a hook in the ceiling of the box. Until my first arrest, I always thought that hook was a purse hanger. The guards unchain the young man and lead him out of the box and back toward the elevators.

"See, I told you it was Robin Green. I'm pretty sure this is his first arrest." The man in front of the line is talking as the infamous subway thief and murderer Robin Green is led past us in shackles. He stares straight ahead and I clench my paper bag close to my chest to stop myself from lunging at him.

"I can't stand that guy. You know I was on two different trains he held up in the future. Stole both my favorite handbags and I had to have my time passport replaced twice when he took my wallets," a woman in line explains to another woman behind her. "It's bad enough the money he stole from me, but those time passports aren't easy to replace. I bounced back and forth between so many offices in this one building, I was about ready to go rogue and get one off the black market." I watch as Green is led onto the elevators and the doors shut behind him.

"Oh, poor you!" the woman's friend replies sarcastically. "I'm sure the stress you had from replacing your little flea-market handbags outweighed all the people who lost their lives when Green shot them to death on those trains."

"Leslie, I didn't mean it like that! And it wasn't my fault those people died. Guard jobs are dangerous and they knew what they were getting into. I didn't sign up to get robbed on my vacation when I bought my ticket." Leslie clicks her tongue at her friend but says nothing more as Green and the guards are long gone and the attendant returns finishing off a bag of chips. He brushes the cheese-flavored dust off his hands and calls out…
"Next!"

Once the line gets moving again I take my place at the end and try to clear my thoughts. Robin Green was a notorious criminal who robbed time trains for a living and killed conductors, guards and passengers as a hobby. According to the rumors he had a black market passport which was, as Leslie's friend implied, much easier to obtain than a legitimate one, which he used to board the trains with various identities. Green's method was to board the train and wait until they were deep in the tunnels about to make a jump through time. When a train was traveling through a time mechanism, depending on the year in which the train was going, the jump could take ten minutes to half an hour through the mechanism. A time frame which made it impossible to use any form of communication or stop the train. Green loved to pick the trains that made big jumps, mostly because it gave him plenty of time to hold up everyone inside while the trains were in a sort of communication blackout. He was known to challenge himself with the occasional quick trips just to see if he could rip people off and beat his previous time. Green had been operating since I was a child. This was actually his first arrest. He had just robbed the train my mother was on that was coming to the first year station. He made it off the train and escaped into one of the portals to another year but was picked up soon after and brought back to the first year just now. No one knew what actual year he was from and I couldn't really tell his age. Maybe early twenties? Looking at him now could still take me back to nightmares of my six-year-old self trapped in a dark and empty station trying to find my Mommy before Green could hurt her. Honestly it didn't make me feel any better to see him get arrested so quickly after his crime, since he will escape before the day is over.

My turn at the box. I step in and press my body against the back wall. There was no one in line behind me, which meant it was almost lunch time. I clutch my paper bag to my chest and stare out the box. Inside the glass is already frosted. It had been so long since I portal jumped and, like flying on a plane after a long time of being on the ground, I forgot how much it scared me until right before take-off. Through the glass I could make out the attendant as he stood at the control panel with his key. There was a man-sized potted tree behind him in the hallway. As I watched the attendant key in the codes and the bulb overhead came to life shining brighter and brighter, I remembered that there were no plants in the hallway when I was in line. The tree seemed to be moving as the light filled the box. The brown limbs flexing on the other side of the frosted glass. I squint trying to make out what I'm seeing. That tree was definitely moving. A burst of light blinds me and I have to shut my eyes. A strong pull in my stomach and I drop my bag to grip the handle bar tight. Then just like that, it's over. The light dims and I open my eyes to see the frost like film melting away off the glass doors. I made it, and I hardly embarrassed my…before I could finish my thought, I was doubled over in the box vomiting.

CHAPTER SIX

I sit in humiliation on a bench in the lobby of the sixth year station trying not to look at the janitor as he closes off the portal box to clean up my mess. Maybe I was getting too old to be jumping through time and my stomach just couldn't handle it anymore? Which was exactly what I told the portal attendant who was adamant on sending me to the station's infirmary. But I just didn't have the time. I declined the offer and signed the stupid waiver not to sue and was on my way to the passport offices.

Passport application offices were on the third floor of the station. The office was packed with people. I thought the lobby at the first year station was crowded, but this was ridiculous. There were ten application windows stretched across the office with only two of the windows actually open for service. One main line stretched down the center of the room and there were at least three dozen plastic chairs circling the room, each filled with someone either working on their paperwork or looking up their own forgotten history on their phone. I claimed my place at the end of the line and waited.

An hour later I approach my window and begin to explain my situation.

"Hello, I'm trying to…"

"Paperwork?" The clerk behind the clear plastic partition isn't even looking at me as she holds her hand out for my passport application. I begin to stutter a reply as I open my paper bag and pull out the crumpled application.

"About my paperwork. I don't actually need a passport…"

"Then why are you here?" The clerk is still looking down at her desk as she writes something and I set the mostly blank application in her free hand.

"Well, I was sent here from the year one station because my release papers…"

"You didn't fill any of this out!" The clerk interrupts and looks at me for the first time after flipping through the papers." You have to fill this out first, and then you get in line." The clerk shoves the papers back through the half-moon hole at the bottom of the window and I grab the pages before they fall off the counter.

"You don't understand, I don't remember all this stuff. I can't fill this out."

"Then you can't get a passport!" The clerk snaps.

"Come on, grandma!" The man behind me tries to push me to the side, and I swing the pages of my application at him.

"Excuse you! You can wait your turn, just like I did." I turn back to the clerk.

"I'm trying to explain to you that I don't need a time passport because I already have one. I was sent here from the year one station to get my travel papers sorted out so I can take my last time trip back home to my own time."

"So you need a replacement time passport? You still have to fill that out!" The clerk argues.

"No, I don't need a replacement! I just need a single pass for a single trip home!"

"It's not that simple, ma'am. This is the office for time passports. If you already have a passport I suggest you use it and go home like a person with some common sense."

"Did you have a senile moment and forget where you left it?" The man behind me asks with a smirk. I clutch my bag tight to my chest and face him.

"No, I didn't lose it. It was revoked, when I went to prison for a time crimes violation. Where I spent ten years repeating the same day over and over again while reliving in my mind the worst day of my life and I'm positive I've accumulated enough bad memories that no amount of senility will make me forget. So I'm very sorry if my complicated situation is bringing you first–world problems, but I'm not going anywhere until I get this sorted out. And if you really want to test me today, I don't mind going back to prison and making new memories of what I do to your face." The entire room falls silent and the man stares at me, his mouth gaping open so far I can see the chewed gum resting on his back teeth. "Now close your mouth and keep quiet while I get my paperwork together." I leave the man stunned and face the clerk who is equally fearful and unsure of what to do next.

"As I was saying, I have a time travel passport, but it was revoked when I was sent to the Preservation. I was released today, but the clerk at the first year station sent me here with this application because she couldn't find the file of my release papers to send me home. All I need from you is a single travel pass which I know the station uses in unusual cases like mine, and I promise you that if you help me, you will never have to see me again since according to my parole this will be my last time jump ever." The clerk stares at me as she bites her lip and without taking her eyes off of me she slowly pulls a sheet of paper from a plastic tray on her desk and begins to fill out the form for me for a single trip pass.

"I'm going to the eightieth year station." I offer as I lean in closer to the window. The clerk nods.

"Yes ma'am!" She whispers quietly.

I wear my best grandmotherly smile, even though I am not a grandmother, as I leave the office with my travel pass in one hand and my paper bag in the other. The pass of course still has to be validated by the Preservation Secretary when I get my release forms all sorted out, but that was one thing I'm happy to be done with and I can't lie, I'm starting to enjoy my elderly criminal persona. No one even had to know what I'd done. But that feeling in the pit of my stomach makes me feel a little guilty for what I'd said. I've never considered myself a violent person and I don't think I could've hurt anyone, but I wanted to do something to that young man and maybe would have done something to him if I were capable and he had pushed me just a little further. Part of me felt wrong, while the other part felt … like I wanted to be satisfied in my anger but just couldn't be. The feeling took me back to when I was a child and my mother tried to explain the Creator's grace over His law to me. She told me one thing told us what not to do, while the other helped us not to do it. A feeling deep inside of you that what you are about to do shouldn't be done and wasn't justified. Of course knowing that never did much for my conscience as an adult, but just then I felt that feeling. The feeling my mother must've been speaking of when I was young. They were words, but I was learning more and more today that my words were a spot-on reflection of all the bad things I didn't want to believe I was capable of.

As I make my way to the nearest portal I stop at a station map in the middle of the lobby to see where I am and where I'm going. According to the map, the portal on this floor is out of service but there is a portal on the fifth floor and I take an escalator to the correct level. As I make my way down the hall past a row of offices I slow down, sure that I can hear my father's voice nearby.

"You have to believe me, my daughter is not a bad kid. She was an honors student before my wife died. She just doesn't know how to deal with her pain…"

"Mr. Ramses, we're not here to talk about your daughter's problems at home. We are talking about what she did right here and right now at this station. Do you have any idea how much damage she could've caused with her so-called prank?" A woman's voice. One I don't recognize. I inch closer to the door and there is my dad sitting in a chair across from a bitter looking woman with a tight face and even tighter hairstyle. Dad looked so worn out over the past six years, so different from the still young father this morning at the first year station. He's got a beard now and his suit is wrinkled. He must've just gotten out of the office when the station called him. This day is coming back to me.

"My daughter is a good kid. There must be some explanation. It's just been hard for her since losing her mother…"

"Which is not an excuse to take out her aggression on this station! She nearly derailed a train with that little joke of hers." Dad runs his fingers through his salt and pepper hair. I didn't realize how my lashing out at the Consortium had changed him. How much all of what I'd done weighed on him. I was too busy being angry at the Creator for the first-world imperfections of my own life. And the closest I could get to venting my hate for the controlling powers was to attack the Consortium. Didn't take long before I lost all direction, but held on to the pain.

"Please, just don't send her to the Preservation. I'll pay for the damages. I'll ground her even, but please don't take her away." Dad is begging and I can't watch anymore.

"Mr. Ramses, please! We don't send children to the Preservation, and thankfully no one was hurt, but like I said this sort of thing cannot be taken lightly. If you don't do something now your daughter's behavior is just going to get worse." I frown and storm down the hall. Not wanting to listen to any more of that. Who was she to judge me? To tell my father that I would just get worse? Of course I did get worse, but that was beside the point! I reach the end of the office and there I am. My twelve-year-old self sitting in an overstuffed chair, still in my school uniform. My legs stretched out in front of me as I play with a single candy wrapper between my fingers. I enter the room slowly and sit down in the chair only two seats over, staring at myself. I'd lost the joy and playful curiosity of my six-year-old self by now. I didn't need dad's old watch to keep me occupied at the station anymore. About a decade from now, after his funeral I would bury it in my jewelry box, and take it out every once in a while to remember the past. I had it in my purse when I was arrested ten years ago, but I don't remember why I even took it out of the house. I stick my hand in my pocket and rub the band thoughtfully.

"Why are you staring at me?" My twelve-year-old self is still looking into her lap, playing with the candy wrapper.

"You look like you've just gotten into some trouble. I know that look." Younger me shrugs without looking up. Trying to pretend she's not scared.

"So what?" She replies simply.

"So what did you do?" With a scowl she fixes her eyes on me.

"None of your business!" Her eyes fall on my wrist and her whole expression changes.

"Whoa! You've been in lockup haven't you?" I touch my wrist and nod.

"I was just released today." Younger me raises an eyebrow questioningly.

"It better not be a fake. I can't see someone like you ending up in the Preservation. You look like you could be my grandma or something."

"No it's true. I did ten years."

"Is it true you repeat the worst times of your life over and over again?"

"You repeat one day over and over again. The worst day. The day you were admitted in the prison is the day you live your entire sentence. That's what the mark is from, the time band everyone has to wear on their wrist." Younger me looks disappointed.

"Aw man, that's not so bad. In school they make it sound like hell on earth or something. Like some kind of purgatory to repeat everything you've ever done wrong until you feel guilty. But it sounds pretty cool to me. You don't age right? It's practically like being immortal or something."

"Not quite. And trust me, if the Preservation is anything close to hell there is nothing cool or interesting about it. You see there's no point in immortality and not aging if there is nothing good you can do with it. Honestly the Preservation is a terrible place. Repeating the same day, the same mistakes, the same conversations and actions … being on repeat can drive a person insane. It's like the station itself; so much time to go over all the things you could've done right and even the opportunity to get it right, but instead you can't help but keep doing everything wrong. People kill themselves in the Preservation because of it. There's nothing fun about that." Younger me falls silent for a moment and drops her candy wrapper.

"What did you do? Why did they arrest you?" I sit back and let her squirm. The little brat I was back then.

"I asked you first." I reply. Younger me slumps lower in her chair and using her outstretched foot she drags the fallen candy wrapper across the floor until she can pick it up again.

"A couple of friends of mine dared me to toss some candy on the tracks." I smile to myself remembering. I wanted so badly to wear my rebellion in front of the other kids. I had a bag of hard candy in my backpack and we took the escalators down to the subway platform. I got as close to the edge as I dared and tossed a handful of sweets down below. I knew all the best ways to lure the kid phantoms. They loved sugar. Sometimes even toys depending on their age. Two phantom boys appeared just as the train was coming in from some timeline. I still remember the sharp squeal of the breaks on the track as the conductor tried to stop in time to avoid hitting what she thought were actual children. In a dark tunnel, if they materialized enough, the phantoms could look … well pretty much like the rest of us. The train couldn't stop fast enough and just before they were hit, the two kids took their candy and disappeared. A guard caught me as we all ran away laughing. Security tried to scare me into thinking I'd go to jail for my prank, claiming the train nearly derailed and killed everyone on board. The passengers were fine, everyone was fine. It was all a load of nonsense scare tactics.

"Don't worry, they sent me away for actual destruction of Consortium and station property. You didn't destroy anything." I explain.

"I wish I had. I wish I had destroyed it all." Younger me whispers, on the brink of tears.

"What's important is that you're going home. That's good news."

"Is it?" She asks and Dad appears.

"Come on, let's go." Dad holds his arm out to her. I smile at him and he nods back barely looking at me. Younger me stands up and Dad wraps his arm around her shoulders. He was trying so hard and it was taking a toll on him. I watch them leave the office, then I continue on my way back to the portal and the first year station.

CHAPTER SEVEN

"What do mean lunch? Still?" I'm standing in the office of the Secretary of Preservation Affairs as the secretary to the Secretary is sitting at his desk typing furiously. The office is filled with at least twenty cubicles, all empty except this one.

"Just what I said. Everyone is still out to lunch. You should've gotten here earlier."

"I couldn't get here any earlier. I was sent to the sixth year station first to get this travel pass." I explain.

"I'm sorry Miss Ramses, but no one can see you right now. People have to eat. Including myself." The man logs off of his computer and closes the books spread across his desk. He stands up and I follow him to the exit.

"Well, hold on a second! What am I supposed to do now? I have to see the Secretary so I can get home. I need my release papers to validate the pass." The man pulls his coat on and reaches into his pocket for a set of keys.

"I would suggest you do the same thing as everyone else and go get something to eat. Someone should be back in an hour and if there is an opening the Secretary can see you."

"And what if there isn't an opening? Then what?" The secretary stops just at the door and stares at me.

"Do you do that often?"

"Do what?" I ask.

"Always consider what might not happen? There might not be an opening. But there might be an opening. Someone like you always looks on the bad side of what if and reacts before anything at all has happened. Actions like that can affect the positive side of any situation and make it less than good news, and it's not very healthy." The secretary opens the door to allow me to exit first. I hate it when a man is gentleman when I want to be angry at him. Elijah used to do that all the time when we argued. I exit the office and stand in the hallway as the secretary follows me then shuts and locks the door.

"You don't understand, I just want to go home." I'm pleading and my poor old lady image isn't doing much to change his mind. With a shrug the secretary of the Secretary turns away and continues down the hall.

"You should get something to eat, Miss Ramses." the secretary calls back from over his shoulder. "You'll feel much better." I sit on a bench in the empty hallway and open my paper bag. Inside is everything I had when I was arrested. Instead of counting how much change I had for lunch. I reach for Milo's seed packet at the bottom of the bag. There is a rust-colored thumbprint on the center of the packet. We were going to visit my parents in the past and Milo wanted to plant a tree. Then that tree would be fully grown when we got back home. But something changed. And in an instant everything was gone. I set the seed packet back in the bag and inhale sharply as I feel something like claws dig into my shoulder. I look back and there is nothing there but the wall. I press my hand to my shoulder and feel blood seeping through the material of my shirt.

"Oh my!" I stand up quickly and search. Above and beneath the seat, scanning the entire wall but there is nothing out of place. What did I cut myself on now? I grab my paper bag and hurry down the hall to the restroom.

I set the bag down on the sink and try to see the blood through my reflection. I can feel a trickle running down my arm. I hold my hand over the sink and try to clean up as far as I can reach.

"What are you doing here?" I look up and there is another of my younger selves standing in the doorway of the restroom. I'm wearing a bright yellow sundress that still barely fits and a pair of white sandals I should've thrown out years ago. I remember this day. I look like I'm going on a first date picnic. If only my plans were so wholesome. I stand up straight, frustrated and toss the paper towel I'd been using to clean up the blood, in the trash. Younger me is confused and somewhat alarmed. I doubt I'm the first future self she's ever seen. And so far she was the third of my past selves I've met today which is unusual even for a time travel station.

"First help me clean this." I reply curtly. I turn my back to my younger self and try to pull my shirt up. Younger me hesitates at first, then relents by grabbing more paper towels and water.

"What happened? How did you get cut?" There is a bit of concern in her voice. Probably wondering if there is some strange altercation in her future? Or just disappointed that at my age I was still getting into scrapes?

"I think I leaned against a nail or something stuck in a wall?" I explain as younger me is cleaning the scratches with cold water. I hiss at her when she digs in a little deep with the paper towel.

"Sorry. These aren't scratches though. At least not from a nail in the wall. And the station is the last place to just leave some random nail sticking out to cut people…"

"Well, I forgot what a know-it-all I used to be. So if you're so smart maybe you can tell me where it's from?" I snap back. Younger me frowns but says nothing at first. She tosses the used towel and I relax when I see there isn't as much blood on the second towel as there was on the first.

"Well, I guess I'd have to know what you were doing when you got cut, wouldn't I?" Younger me is leaning on the sink staring at me as I fix my blouse and look away. Actually I was staring at her reflection in the mirror trying to remember her age as I explain that I was just sitting on a bench minding my own business trying to get home when I felt something in my shoulder. I didn't mention the previous scratches on my ankle though.

"You were just sitting on a bench, alone in a hallway when something … scratched you?" Younger me is scrutinizing my story with confusion.

"That's what I said." I reply exhausted.

"It sounds a little strange. And there was nothing on the wall or behind you? Was there even a nail?" She asks.

"If there was a nail I would've been sure of what cut me." I explain, not holding back my annoyance. Just because I was older, didn't mean I was delusional.

"Sorry, I didn't mean to ask such an obvious question but even you have to admit it sounds strange. Were you cut anywhere else?" I look away as I answer.

"No, just my back." My ankle was an accident somewhere. It wasn't the same thing so she didn't need to know about it. She shrugs, knowing that I'm lying but doesn't say anything more about it.

"Well, I've helped you clean up, so now you can tell me what you're doing here? I've never seen myself at the station before." She explains, which is likely a lie.

"Neither have I." I reply, which is definitely a lie. And there's that feeling in my conscience again.

"Well?" She waits and I begin to wash my hands as I'm thinking.

"I'm trying to go home but there was a slight problem and I had to get a travel pass for the day since I don't have my passport at the moment." I explain vaguely.

"The Consortium doesn't give out day passes in place of a passport." I flash the pass and surprise my younger self.

"They do for lost little old ladies like us."

"You mean like you." Younger me replies as I put the travel pass back in my paper bag for safe keeping.

"Anyway, why are you here? What year are you?" I retort as younger me is checking her make-up in the mirror. She begins to smooth out her dress and tug gently at the fabric as it's a little too tight around the waist but it was Micah's favorite color.

"You know what year I am, just like you know why I'm here. You lived it already."

"You don't know that. I could be a different future than the one you'll see and you might be a completely different past than the one I've lived." Younger me rolls her eyes.

"Give me a break. You know our timeline is the same. Nothing's changed except this right here. Unless you're lying about this meeting in your past? And that sounds like something I would do." I shake my head slowly.

"I'm not lying. I didn't meet any of my other selves when I was you. I don't even remember going to the bathroom at the station that day. But then again, my intentions left me a little unfocused." Younger me makes a face at my reflection.

"I don't care what you say. I'm going through with this. It will work."

"I didn't say it wouldn't or that it didn't. Whatever it is?"

"Don't mess with me, old woman. You had the same ideas back then that I have now so don't judge me. I want a baby. I want a family. Elijah and I both want a family."

"So, he's still around?' I interject and heartbreak is read across her face. I'd said something on purpose just to be cruel and I continue, pretending I don't notice.

"And you're on your way to see Micah five years in the past so you must be thirty…six-year-old me, right?"

"What do you mean by 'so he's still around?" Elijah and I love each other. He wouldn't leave me."

"You and Micah loved each other, too."

"That was different…"

"No, it wasn't." Younger me struggles to hold back any further emotional reaction so as not to ruin her make-up job. She'd gone to a lot of work to smooth out the last five years on her face, even dying her hair to cover the premature graying.

"It was different. Micah and I didn't want the same thing. At least not at the same time. I did love him … I do love him, but he couldn't make up his mind. He claimed he didn't want responsibility when we were together. Just wanted us to be free and in love; so, no kids. And then we divorce, and now he's got two beautiful babies with his new wife just a few years later and another one on the way and I'm getting older and trying to make it work with Elijah but … I love Lij, and he'll make a great father, but right now we need Micah to do what Elijah can't. I'm sure you understood it when you lived it?"

"Not really, but I wanted to. I really wanted logic and reason to overcome my conscience and what little sense of morality I had back then. So I can understand the effort, but not the goal." Younger me stands her ground though.

"But it works, doesn't it?" She asks calmly, knowingly.

"It does." I answer and she wipes her eyes delicately.

"Good. That's all that matters then."

"Is it?" Younger me shrugs.

"Elijah might leave and he might not. Like you said, your past might not exactly be my present if something changed. And if he does leave … well, I can't make his life decisions for him. I'd rather raise my child in a house that's whole but …" Younger me stares at me. "Is it a boy or girl? No, wait, don't tell me. I want to be surprised."

"You will be." I say grimly. Younger me examines herself again as I grab my paper bag and head for the exit.

"Well, have a safe trip home and try to be more careful around nails or whatever." I nod and exit the restroom, not wanting to look at her anymore

CHAPTER EIGHT

I had to get out of there. I still had just over half an hour before anyone got back to the Secretary's office and even that felt like an eternity. So I went back to the portal. I had to occupy my mind with something. I would take a jump somewhere and waste time and hopefully when I got back I would see the Secretary and get out of this ridiculous place. But where would I go? As far as I could for now. I didn't want to be here. I didn't want to be anywhere near the me that was going to do what I was going to do. Even for the reasons I was going to do them. I approach the box and the attendant asks me where I want to go.

"How far can I go? How far in the future can I go? I mean, in the station's future?" The attendant looks at me curiously.

"Well, it depends. I mean how far do you want to go? You can go as far as you want." She explains.

"But what's the furthest? I mean what's the furthest year I can possibly travel to?" I'd only used the portals occasionally in my youth and I never wondered before just how far I could jump. How far is far enough?

"Ma'am, this would be so much easier if you would just pick a year. I mean, you're holding up the line." A number comes to mind.

"Okay, I want to go to the one-hundredth year." The attendant smiles and turns to the keypad.

"Okay perfect…" As the attendant begins to key in a number, I interrupt.

"Wait, no … I want to go to the one-hundred and twentieth year." Less excited by my change the attendant nods and begins again.

"Okay, got it."

"No … wait no, I don't want that one. How about the hundred and fiftieth year?" The attendant is annoyed now.

"Ma'am, everyone knows the portals don't go that far."

"Obviously not everyone knows that because I didn't. You could've told me that when I asked how far I could go." The attendant pastes a fake smile on her face and explains.

"Well, I apologize but most travelers already know this. Anything further than year one forty-nine is only accessible through the subway system." I give a fake smile back.

"Well, I guess I'm not most travelers. I'd like to go to the one-hundred and forty-ninth station …please?" The attendant sets the date as I step into the box. What was I going to do that far in the future? I close my eyes and the doors shut and I let the box do its thing.

At least I didn't throw up this time. But I was about ready to fight that last attendant as soon as the one outside the box announced… "Welcome to the fortieth station!" Somehow I knew that last portal attendant would mess with me like this. I exit the portal and enter the lobby of the fortieth station. I had already been to this station-year for a meeting I could go without reliving, but I immediately hit the elevators and make my way to the first floor anyway. Then the escalators that lead to the subway platform and the tunnels below. The platforms are divided into quadrants for north, south, east and west divisions of the globe. Trains for each specified quadrant only make trips for that specified area of the globe but can take a traveler to any time period in that division, down to the hour of choice. The tunnels are constructed on an incline which leads to the core of the station where the time mechanism is housed. A train arrives every half hour to jump either forward or back, alternating with each train. Depending on how far back a person wanted to go, they could save money on an indirect ticket and book a connecting travel, catching a train at the next station, or multiple trains at multiple stations. I watched from a distance as passengers flipped their passports out to be scanned at the turn-style and allow a person to enter the actual platform to wait for an approaching train. I prop myself up against a wall and watch the travelers. Hoping this is not the day or the hour I remember. Sometimes Dad and I would meet Mom on the platform when I was very young, why couldn't I see one those moments again?

"Ow! What is wrong with this thing?!" A young woman is caught in the barrier. She scans her passport again across the machine but the barrier still won't move.

"You have to be kidding me! I'm going to miss my train! I know it's those stupid kids!" And just like that, two twin girls appear holding the barrier in place and laughing hysterically. The woman attempts to brush the kids away like a fly but her arm goes right through one as she disintegrates then solidifies again still holding the barrier in place. A candy bar slides across the floor, stopping just at the woman's feet.

The phantom girls release the barrier and reach for the chocolate bar at the same time. I'd never seen the phantoms eat but they could pick things up, like candy, and they usually ran off with their bounty to parts unknown. The woman quickly scans her passport again and the barrier opens allowing her to enter the platform.

"Thanks." The woman nods to the older woman a few feet away who threw the candy. The older woman shrugs.

"No problem."

"You did more than those lazy guards over there." The woman continues speaking as she enters the platform and takes her seat to wait for the oncoming train. The young woman is gone but the older woman with the candy and her male companion still haven't entered the platform. I watch the woman as she watches the phantom twins fighting over their chocolate bar before disappearing.

"Can we get back to our conversation please?" The male companion snaps at the woman and she returns her attention to him.

"I'm not going to apologize for anything. I love my son." The woman explains.

"Oh, now he's your son. But when it comes to money he's our son. And I don't expect you to apologize for anything because out of all the selfish things you've done in your life, you've never apologized for a single thing. And it wouldn't mean anything to me anyway."

"I'm just asking for a little help…" The woman begins, but the man cuts her off.

"You're not asking for anything! You're suing me for child support for a child I never knew about. How old is this kid? Ten? Eleven? And what's even worse is how he came to be in the first place. You're lucky I don't press charges against you!"

"You can't press charges against me for anything! I didn't commit a crime."

"You took advantage of me El!" The platform falls silent as Micah's voice echoes through the tunnels. Embarrassed, my younger self searches the underground space for a more private location to continue their conversation.

"Can we not do this in public?" She asks.

"Oh, now you're embarrassed? Now you want privacy? You didn't respect my privacy! You didn't respect my choices!"

"What choices? You told me you didn't want children and now you have three kids by that woman…" Younger me is trying to plead her case.

"I choose who I start a family with! I choose! I started a family with the woman I love and I had every right to!" I think my heart broke a little more than hers just then. The first time I heard it I thought maybe he said it in anger but as time went by and I remembered it afterward I realized he meant every word of it.

"We both moved on and you can't hold me responsible for what your new guy couldn't or wouldn't do. You wanted a family; you could've had it with him somehow. You did this out of spite and you know it."

"The hearing is next month. I'll see you at the year one station then." Younger me exits the platform.

"You don't even care what this is doing to my family, do you? My wife looks at me like I had an affair or something. It's like you have no morals, El!" Micah kicks his duffel bag which is resting on the ground as younger me walks away. She passes me on her way to the escalators and we make eye contact. She stops at the foot of the steps then continues on without saying anything. I watch her until she disappears at the top and enters the lobby. Micah takes his bag and scans his passport and enters the platform to return home to his family.

She's waiting for me at a coffee kiosk when I reach the lobby. Younger me is sitting a few feet from the kiosk at a table with two chairs and two cups of coffee. I take a chance and sit across from her.

"What are you doing here?" She asks. Honestly I didn't know. Something very strange was going on. But I shrug instead and thank her for the coffee.

"Strange you would just show up on the platform to see that."

"Why was he here?" Younger me drinks her coffee silently at first.

"After I filed for child support Micah said I had made it all up. That I couldn't possibly have a son by him. He came to this time to see Milo and I took him to the school and from only a few feet away he could see. He could see that was his son. He still didn't understand until the ride back to the station when he remembered the last time we were together, before he filed for divorce." Younger me looks me directly in the eyes.

"Was he already seeing her by then?" She asks sincerely. I shake my head and drink my coffee.

"I thought so, once or twice. But now I don't think so. I really think he just fell out of love, if he ever was in love with us? Or maybe he thought he was and it was just a youthful mistake." Younger me looks away in anger.

"That doesn't make me feel better." She replies.

"It wasn't meant to. I just wanted to be honest."

"You know in the times of the Creator marriage was supposed to be until death. When you married and gave your body to someone you were bound to them in a sealed unity. A covenant that was so strong no man could separate them. But even then I guess a good divorce attorney was no mere man."

"I'm sure that's what we like to believe." I mumble to myself more so but she hears me anyway.

"What do you believe? Has anything in you changed since you were me?" I look myself directly in the eye in return and nod.

"I'm starting to believe that maybe life isn't so easy to predict now. And that the decisions I've made were not the best for me and even worse for the people close to me. I believe we spent so long trying to drive life in a direction we wanted that we didn't really live. The things we were in a rush to get I still haven't grasped at my age and the things I wanted to avoid I'm experiencing all the more."

"You sound like you miss the Creator?" Younger me says with mild humor.

"You sound like you believe He left." I reply and she frowns.

"I don't believe He left. Honestly I don't believe He was ever here considering how things were before. And now with the innovations that we have today, we don't need to rely on what doesn't exist. People can look to themselves now. If we make a mistake we can go back and fix it. If we fear the future we can go forward and see."

"Sounds like time travel has been working out real good for you?" I reply sarcastically.

"You can't blame a person for using what's around them to get what they want. You lived this life too, remember? You made the same choices I made. And involved the same people."

"And look how far it got me." I hold my wrist in the air revealing the mark I was trying to keep hidden under my sleeve. Her eyes widen in fear.

"Is that a Preservation mark? What did we do to end up in the Preservation?" She whispers.

"You mean which one of our various crimes lost us ten years? Pick one? It shouldn't even matter."

"Of course it matters! Losing ten years in the Preservation matters!" Younger me is getting loud and a few patrons nearby look up annoyed. Embarrassed, younger me tries to calm herself down.

"Sorry!" She begins speaking to me in a whisper. "It does matter…"

"Does it matter enough for you to not do what you've done so far? Does it matter enough for you to give up Milo? To even wish you'd never done what you did to have him? Does it matter enough for you to go back to your youth and talk to Dad, tell him how you feel? Tell him about the anger inside of you over Mom's death? Instead of taking your anger out on the station? Does it matter enough to you to stop this ridiculous crusade of revenge against the Consortium? Does it matter enough to you to be the humble one and admit that even you think things wouldn't be this bad for us under the Creator?" Younger me rests back in her chair and looks away saying nothing.

"Of course not." I continue. "So while it matters, it doesn't matter enough to overcome your pride. It doesn't matter enough to set aside revenge. It doesn't matter enough to wait for the right time."

"I've spent enough time waiting."

"If you think you've spent enough time at that, what you were doing wasn't waiting at all."

"Are you going to give me a sermon now? You hated waiting on the Creator to do something in your life. To give you at least one thing that you've wanted in life."

"You're right. I did. Until I realized some of the things I wanted in life were for the wrong reasons and some things were so much better for me to not have at all. But I didn't know that when I wanted them. And most of my waiting was spent believing that what I wanted wasn't coming at all, while ignoring all the good things I already had. A delay is not always a no. Sometimes something needs to be gained in a time it's perfect for."

"I still want you to tell me why we go to the Preservation?" I finish my cup of coffee and stand up. Younger me grabs my arm and we both pull back, shocked at the electric force of our touch. My arm burns and I rub it gently as I think of replacing a light bulb and have no idea why that thought comes to mind.

"Tell me why! Maybe I can do something different." I remain on my feet, pushing my chair in.

"You can't and you won't do anything different. What happens is going to happen and nothing ever changes. You can't prepare for it, you just go through it."

"I don't want to go through it!' Younger me is terrified. "I'm tired of going through it! I'm tired of things not fitting together like they should. I fall in love but we're going in two different directions. So we separate. I marry another great guy and we want the same thing until we get it and suddenly he doesn't want it anymore. I'm tired of living in an era like this and still feeling like I'm running out of time. I'm tired of struggling. And I'm tired of surprises. What did we do to end up in the Preservation?!" I stare at myself and see the distress in her eyes. She still sees death on the horizon. My forties were a bad time for me, for reasons that I mentioned earlier that I wouldn't talk about. But it's strange that even after seeing me, she still believes her life is almost over.

"You get what you want. Or what you think you want. Micah pays the child support. Every month, he's never late. But those payments are the closest you'll ever get to him again."

"And Milo? What's going to happen to him? Where is he when we're in prison?" I try my best to lie to her but I can't form the words, so instead I turn and walk away.

"Oh God!" She bows her head to the table and begins to cry. I don't stop and I don't look back again. I need to get to the nearest portal.

After Elijah and I separated I struggled to take care of Milo on my own. And Milo's behavior, his emotions became too much to bear at times. I wanted to take my frustration out on someone and Micah was right. I did what I did out of spite. He was happy and I wasn't. And we were supposed to be happy together and that didn't work out. I thought if only he would change his mind and … well, I don't know what I thought. But, whatever it was, it ruined too many relationships. Micah's wife Rebecca left him two years after that encounter at the station. Milo was twelve, when he should've been about seventeen. Milo was conceived before Micah and I began our divorce, one year before he married Rebecca. I made the jump forward to my own time right after I tricked Micah which meant Milo wasn't born until five years after he was conceived. When his two half siblings were somewhere around three and two, so I could see why Rebecca was less than understanding and possibly very confused. I leave the lobby feeling even worse than when I arrived. I return to the portal, then the first year station for my meeting.

This time the office of the Secretary is full of people. Each cubicle had at least two or three people hovering over a computer or watching a television monitor playing videos of Green's capture and arrest. I pause in front of a screen suspended from the ceiling long enough to watch the grainy video footage of Green's tiny figure being dragged off the train and thrown on the platform when he tried to flee again through the subway system. He didn't even put up a fight. Where was all his bravado now? He was so complacent on the ground, and smirking? He was actually smirking! Trying to hold up the genius thief appearance as if he planned his own capture or something. What a clown! I turn away in disgust as everyone else is still buzzing about how much time he would get and how it would all be handled in the media. As if some people could breathe easier knowing someone like him was off the tracks, so to speak. It didn't change anything. There would always be people like Robin Green, even they had their purpose. I approach the same desk as earlier and find the same secretary to the Secretary typing furiously.

"Welcome back Miss Ramses. How was your lunch?" the secretary asks without taking his eyes off the computer screen.

"Just peachy." He smiles and motions for me to take a seat.

"The Secretary is in a meeting at the moment but I can squeeze you in when he's finished."

"Thank you. I don't think I would've come back had you not suggested it."

"Power of positive words. Sorry about the hectic office. Everyone's all animated about Robin Green's capture."

"I see." I stare straight ahead at a television monitor on the wall replaying the arrest. After robbing the train my mother was on, Robin took a portal jump to the fiftieth year station and tried to board a subway line. But there was a glitch in the black market passport he was using. For every trip Green used a new throwaway passport but this time he must've gone to the wrong provider. Green was hog-tied and carried by five guards back up to the lobby.

"Were you ever on a train he robbed?" the secretary asks. I shake my head.

"No, but my mother was. She used to work for the Consortium and she liked to ride the trains with the travelers. One day she boarded the wrong one."

"Really? Poor woman. She must've been terrified?"

"I'm sure she was." I say quietly. Three people in suits exit the office behind me and the secretary picks up the phone.

"Miss Ramses is here to see you." The secretary nods and smiles at me as he sets the phone down.

"He'll see you now. It's the blue door behind you."

"Thank you again." I stand up and take my bag with me as I enter the office.

CHAPTER NINE

The office is nondescript like the Secretary himself. A man younger than me, but still old. No pictures, no plaques on the desk or walls. Just a single degree from a college I'd never heard of and a computer. We greet each other and for some reason I expected something bigger, someone bigger. The kind of person who felt the need to exert his authority with a chair larger than mine and a huge desk full of mementos of his conquests in the race of global authority and supremacy. To be honest I was a little disappointed. Mostly at myself for being so intimidated by this man who seemed so much more frightening when his true form was hidden behind the curtain. He motions for me to take a seat and I comply. As I sink into the cushions I realize just how tired my body is. I'd done four portal jumps in a single day and encountered four of my former selves where all but one was less than encouraging. I still had no record of my release and couldn't go home. And it was barely midday.

"So, Ms. Else Ramses. It is nice to meet you in person. I'm fairly familiar with your file and I've been notified that there was some trouble in locating your release papers from the Preservation."

"Yes. Thank you for squeezing me in today. I would really like to get home as soon as possible."

"I understand. I do have one question first Ms. Ramses? When did you arrive here?" I think for a moment.

"I believe it was early this morning. I'm not sure exactly of the time but the sun was up." I smile uncomfortably. I really had no idea what time I had arrived but why did it even matter? Why didn't he just look up my paperwork?

"Is there something wrong with my release?" I ask fearfully. The Secretary begins to rub his hands together.

"Well that's just it. We have no release of you on file. We had no Preservation transport to the station this morning and if we had it would've been a bit more formal then just dropping you off in the center of the lobby." I grip my bag and stare out the window. I know I remember a bus and being dropped off at the station. If I hadn't been released where did I get my ticket from? I reach into my bag and pull the ticket out.

"This is all a mistake. I must've been released. I was given a ticket." I hand the ticket to the Secretary and he studies it silently before handing it back to me.

"Well this is all very confusing…"

"Can't you just contact the Preservation? They must have everything on file! It's not as if I could just walk out!" The Secretary nods and pulls a file out of a drawer.

"Yes, we thought of that. They also have no record of your release."

"That's impossible! How else would I have gotten out?! I did my ten years. My sentence was served…"

"Ms. Ramses, please calm down…"

"I won't calm down. You're telling me that I didn't do something that I know I did and that I wasn't released when I know I was and what? What happens now? I just want to go home."

"Go home to what?" the Secretary asks. "You have no family. Nothing and no one to take guardianship over you as you serve your parole. And how do we know you won't just return to the station in your own time and commit another crime? I mean you're not exactly reformed."

"Who are you to tell me that? I'm not a child, you know. I served my time and I want nothing more to do with this station. I want nothing more to do with the Consortium or the Preservation. I've learned from my mistakes."

"I'd like to believe that." The Secretary is still holding the file.

"So why don't you?"

"Because of the obvious. You're not reformed. You're unrepentant in every way. You commit another crime that has severe consequences for this Consortium and this station." The room grows cold and my chest hurts, like I can't quite get enough oxygen.

"First off, I'm going home, and second, I wouldn't and couldn't do anything anymore severe than what I've done already. And you can't judge me for a crime I commit in the future. That's illegal and even this

Consortium is not above the law. As much as you all act like it is." The Secretary frowns.

"The purpose of this Consortium was to revive a failed world and replace a belief system that was lacking in all points. Caution for this Consortium usurps natural and governing laws. The accumulation of all your crimes proves to be more than just a financial loss for us."

"All of my crimes? What do you mean all of my crimes? And the biggest failure of this world is the Consortium itself!" The Secretary reopens the folder to a specific page and hands the file across the desk. I scan the documents and see my whole life again. Full of every mistake I've made, down to the most shaming details. Most frightening is that some of what is listed in the file, I don't even remember doing.

"What is this? I wasn't charged with any of this and I didn't break any real laws! These were mistakes! Mistakes you don't have the right to punish me for."

"It may not be against the law according to our government to go back in time and trick your ex-husband into impregnating you while you're married to your new husband in your own time years later, but it is a crime against human morality and I'm sure the old Creator wouldn't smile upon it either, if you believed in that sort of thing."

"You're actually throwing morality in my face and judging my actions. You work for an oppressive organization in which morality is a foreign word. Along with compassion, humility, altruism, modesty, honor, integrity. The list can go on all day."

"Now who is being the hypocritical one? You're angry at the Consortium for the decisions you made on your own like all those who blamed their wonderful Creator if they got so much as a paper cut. There is a big wide world out there that does not revolve around one single person and the choices you've made have effects on the people with the hard luck of being around you. No one forced you to do what you did or how. No one else made you leave your second husband. Then when the money runs dry on your own, you and you alone had the audacity to sue your ex-husband for child support, to support a child you tricked him into having in the first place, that he didn't even know about. You have no guilt whatsoever to that, but you want to talk to me about things like honor and integrity and tell me you're reformed." I felt like I was about to vomit. I push the file away and stare out the window.

"You have no right to throw those things in my face. They were personal issues."

"Which had not so personal consequences for the station. You used Consortium property to create a human life. A human life that your bitterness killed."

"Shut up!" I hiss and the room goes cold and still. My eyes begin to burn and I pull tissues out of the box on the edge of the desk so hard the box falls to the floor.

"You can't use this to send me back! You can't do that and I will fight it!"

"That's not why you're going back to the Preservation. With the crimes you've committed it was necessary to examine your future actions. As I said before you do something … that could be catastrophic to the Consortium and this station," His words sit uncomfortably with me as I am leaning out of my chair to pick up the tissue box. I set the box on the desk and wipe my eyes as the Secretary continues.

"If left unchecked. We can't leave that unchecked. We had hoped to change the course of the future with your prison sentence and, in my opinion, you deserved much more than a decade for the lives you've ruined. The High Court took a chance in your 'reformation' by creating situations in which … in which they had hoped for a change. But that won't work either. We have to send you back to save the Consortium and the future of the station." I sit back in the chair defiantly as a guard appears beside me. I hadn't even heard him come in.

"Is this some kind of joke? I served my time and now no one can confirm my release but here I am. And you're trying to send me back to that pit for crimes I haven't even committed? The future is not definite. Half the things listed in here I don't even remember." The guard begins to lift me by the arm out of my seat.

"You can't do this! I can't be imprisoned for future crimes! The future isn't even set!" I'm led out of the office to a silent lobby. The entire outer office has been cleared. The desk of the secretary to the Secretary is also empty. I had no idea the Consortium was even keeping track of everything I'd done, or would do. Or that it would matter this much that they'd go the extent of breaking their own laws just to arrest me again.

A detaining cell on the sixth floor has become another home away from home for me. I'm in a small cell two spaces over from my younger self. Technically me, pre-Preservation and ten years my junior, smoldering with quiet defiance to cover her broken heart.

"What are you staring at?" she asks. Younger me is filthy. Covered in soot and blood. Her knuckles are shredded raw, three fingers broken. I rub my withered hands gently, remembering when I tried to dig Milo out of the rubble of the collapsed tunnel.

"I'm sorry for what happened," I reply. Younger me is confused. Realizing who I am and trying to comprehend why we look near identical, she prepares to ask but can't seem to decide on her first question.

"I'm ten years ahead of you, from the eightieth year."

"Why don't you look older?" She asks.

"Ten years in the Preservation. That's what we're sentenced to after Milo's … after his death. Ten years of repeating the same day and not aging."

"They're going to send me to the Preservation for something that I couldn't even control?" I shrug.

"It gets worse than that. I'm you when we're released and we've only been out a day and they're sending us back." Younger me looks alarmed.

"What? Why?" She asks.

"For a crime we haven't committed yet…"

"They can't do that! A person can't be tried for crimes they haven't committed yet." Younger me explains as if we don't already know.

"They can and have. Just like how they can give you ten years for Milo's suicide. They can and will."

"Milo didn't commit suicide," she explains. "He fell off the platform."

"Else! You know perfectly well that he jumped."

"He did not jump! My boy did not jump! He wanted to live. He wanted to see his grandparents. I was taking him to see Mom and Dad." Younger me begins to cry and rests her head in her hands. "I thought if I could just…" Crying uncontrollably, younger me stops, and I finish.

"I know what you thought. That if he could meet Mom and Dad he might finally feel like he belonged somewhere. He might want to stay. He might have a reason to stay."

"He looked at me. He looked right at me and he kissed me on the cheek and I saw the seed packet in his hands. The one from when he was a kid and I couldn't get a passport for him. I was about to ask him why he still had the seeds and I could feel the train approaching. I could feel it in my toes, my feet, even my whole body, and like that he was gone." Younger me stares at her damaged hands. "I tried to dig him out. After everything collapsed I woke up and I thought I heard him calling me from under the rubble. I just started digging and the fire department was there and they said he was gone."

"He is gone. He's dead, Else."

"I deserve to go to prison then. It was my fault. His whole life was my fault. I deserve those ten years," younger me admits.

"Nobody deserves losing ten years to that place. I'd take a normal prison over the Preservation any day. And we didn't mean any harm doing what we did. We couldn't have known what was going to happen."

"We could've known, if we'd listened to someone but we didn't listen to anyone because we didn't care. And what do you know about anything anyway? You just said it yourself that you're going right back. And for what? A crime you haven't even committed yet!"

"I think I might have destroyed some part of the station? The Secretary of Preservation Affairs said I'd done something that could be catastrophic for the Consortium. I mean what could I do to them? Maybe I messed with the portals somehow." I rub my arm, still feeling the electric tingle where the younger me grabbed me in the café. Why had I thought of changing a bulb? Like the one in the portal box?

"I've always hated this station. It's not life, it's death here. Time travel, what a joke. Not enough time in the world to undo the mistakes we've made. And for what? For what?"

"Robin Green destroyed our family, not the station." I correct my younger self and she doesn't take it lightly.

"Robin Green is a creation of this station! A lowlife pig like Green would never have been on the same train as our mother had it not been for this station. A Robin Hood of the future. Stealing from the rich and giving to himself. You know people actually worship that animal for what he does. Robbing people! They think it's cool, noble. He stole my mother from me! Shot her in cold blood over a stupid necklace. But it is this station that … I can't explain it, but whatever we do to it that's so catastrophic will be the one thing in my life that I don't regret." Younger me is crying and furious. I bury deep inside of me the emotion she's showing so freely now. I had saved up my allowance to buy mom a necklace. The stone was fake, but it sparkled and she loved it. She wore it on the train one day and maybe in his rush to grab and go, Green mistook it for a real stone. Witnesses said mom tried to explain that it's only value was sentimental and Green went into a rage and shot her dead. All the pranks started a few years later. Things I did to fill the void and hide my anger.

"Death and loss have always been around. Long before this station. You act like the Creator would've stopped mom's death. At least this way we can still see her with a jump to the past. Before our time, death was just death. There was no after," I explain.

"Before our time, death was the end that warned us to enjoy life while we had it. And to choose good things," younger me counters. "Not to go chasing after things we've already done and seen because we're too afraid of something new. And from what I remember the Creator didn't bring death, the serpent did. Along with sin and ego and everything else that drove us to wanting to be gods, because being made in His image alone didn't suffice." I go still and stare at my hands.

"Do you remember being arrested before today?" I ask my younger self. She looks at me and considers the question then shakes her head.

"No. But I figure the Preservation is very weird so maybe I was and just don't remember." I chew my lip as I try to figure this out.

"The Secretary said I committed more crimes. And the file he showed me said I … we had been arrested more than once. I don't remember being arrested before either. He said we were on house arrest after the candy prank on the tracks."

"What candy prank?" younger me asks. I explain about what happened when we were twelve and younger me stares at me blankly.

"I don't remember that at all."

"I vaguely remembered it at first. But I saw myself with Dad earlier today in another year of the station after I'd been caught and it all came back to me. Dad was terrified that they would send me away." Younger me is still confused.

"But I don't remember that at all. Are you sure?"

"I…' I open my mouth to respond and realize that I'm not sure. I remembered the candy incident but not until after I traveled to that year. Like a memory that wasn't a memory but a suggestion of one. "Why are you in a cell at the first year station?" I ask my younger self. She shrugs.

"After the tunnel collapsed they arrested me. I didn't even know why until you showed up. I should be asking you why you're here?"

"But we weren't at the first year station when Milo jumped.' Younger me pauses and stares at her broken hands again. "Your wounds are fresh. Like it just happened but it didn't happen here. And I wasn't arrested right after. I was in the hospital first. I remember being in a hospital first. Then I was charged and brought here for trial. My hands had started to heal by then. So why are you here now?" The lights overhead begin to flicker as younger me looks as confused as I am. The room goes pitch black and I hear myself inhale sharply. A moment later the lights come back on and younger me is gone. The cell empty of any trace of her. I stand up and grab the bars. There is a camera in the corner ceiling of the room. I stare into it trying to understand what is going on? This has never happened before. Encountering five of my past selves in the places they shouldn't be and now I was questioning my own memories.

"I remember encountering myself once and only once before." I speak directly at the camera to whoever is watching on the other side. Assuming there is a speaker or a microphone somewhere in the room. "And I swore that I would never encounter myself again. So I may not know what you are doing but I know that this is you. This is all The Consortium. And whatever it is, it won't work." The bright red light of the camera blinks in response and the power goes out again. Now I knew something was off. There had never been a power outage at the station before. And now we'd just had two. I can hear a strange hiss overhead followed by an equally strange smell tickling my nostrils. I cover my nose with my shirt and stare into the darkness just outside my cell as my eyes adjust and I try to follow the movement in the corner. I hear the sound of something like twigs snapping as items begin to fall to the floor. It's coming closer to my cell and I back away from the bars just as rope like roots pour across the floor toward me and slip through the bars of the holding cell. I climb onto the bench in the corner and watch the massive roots spread and reach for me. My eyes trail along the roots back out into the darkness and the outline of a massive tree in the shadows draws closer to the cell door. A large root wraps around the bars of the door and the entire cell begins to groan as I feel myself getting dizzy. They were pumping some kind of gas into the room. I lose my balance on the bench as the roots wrap tighter around the cell door. Whatever was after me has finally caught up with me. I collapse on the bench and lose consciousness.

CHAPTER TEN

When I awake the tree and its roots are gone. The lights are still off but my cell looks unchanged and the room seems as it should be except there are two dead men in uniform sprawled on the floor just outside of my holding cell. The only light is coming from the emergency lights overhead. I sit up a little too quickly and the darkened room begins to spin. I shut my eyes and brace myself against the wall. I don't know how long I'd been asleep or why the gas had been pumped into the room in the first place. When the power comes back on and I can see the destruction more clearly. Blood on the walls and the floor. And a few bullet holes. There had been a fight obviously, or a very unbalanced duel. The door leading into the guard's office was open slightly but I couldn't see anyone outside.

"Hello?!" I call out but no response. Except for the crackle of a radio on the belt of one of the dead men.

"Green's heading for the tunnels! Proceed with caution." Green again? I thought he was long gone. Had they brought him in while I was unconscious and he took his chance? Had this been how he escaped originally? Whatever happened there was no point in me standing around like a fool. I didn't want to go back to the Preservation and if I didn't get out of here now I might miss my chance. I pull a set of keys off of the guard nearest me and after four tries I find the right key to open my cell.

The guard's office is empty like I thought. Papers strewn everywhere, broken furniture. More bullet holes and blood and at least five or six more dead guards. An entire wall of monitors with various screens blacked out.

"Green's in the North tunnel!" Another radio on a desk updates me of where the guards are going. I wait listening closely for more but there is only silence. What was in the tunnels? Where was Green going? I leave the radio and search the set of lockers on the wall for my belongings. My paper bag is worn out but holding together. I reach in the bag for the packet of seeds sitting at the bottom. I roll the top of the bag shut and try to figure out what to do next. As long as everyone was distracted by Green I needed to find a way out of the station. With my bag I head for the exit but stop short. There is a portal key hanging over the door. I rip the key off the cord and leave the office.

The entire floor is empty. Even the portal is unmanned. Except for a teenage phantom girl sitting on the bench beside the portal. We make eye contact as I approach the box and stick the key in but hesitate. Was it Green who had left the key? Even stranger than if he had, why did I take it? This could all still be a part of the game the Consortium was playing?

"Don't be scared, if you fall I'll catch you." I look up sharply at the phantom girl as she has reappeared on the bench. I've never heard a phantom speak. I've heard them make noises like laughter and burping, coughing and sneezing. I once heard one with the hiccups. A little boy that would disappear and reappear with each hiccup. It was amusing watching him cross the station platform blinking in and out of existence. "Did you say something?" I ask the girl and she stands up. Without seeing her move she appears beside me. She turns the key and enters the portal code. She enters the seventieth year and I shake my head.

"I can't go back there. That's the year I'm arrested. It's the year Milo dies." The girl smiles at me and points to the box.

"What is happening?" I ask her. Instead of answering, the girl points to the elevator. The numbers are lit up and someone is coming. Without waiting for an answer I jump into the open portal box. The phantom girl turns the key again and the doors to the portal shut just as the elevator opens and two guards exit. They see me in the box and begin running toward me. The girl smiles at me and says something just as she presses the button. I watch her lips move before she vanishes and the approaching guards become blurred by the frost thickening over the glass doors. The overhead light fills the small space and I shut my eyes.

CHAPTER ELEVEN

I land in the crowded lobby of the seventieth station. I exit the box and ignore the attendant greeting me with fake cheer. The date above the box is one week after Milo killed himself. I believe I was in the Preservation by now. Or at least the me that I was supposed to be. I was having trouble concentrating on the timeline. My mind still focusing on what the phantom girl said to me. It was so surprising to hear her talk that I was beginning to think I hadn't heard her at all. Had I just heard my own thoughts running through my head? "Don't be scared. I'll catch you if you fall." Now I have to stop. I rush into a nearby restroom and shut myself in a stall. My paper bag gets caught on the lock and rips open as I try the pull the bag free. The items inside land on the clean tile floor. The packet of seeds glides across the tile and hits the base of the toilet. Don't be scared. I'll catch you if you fall. I'd said that to Milo when he was only five years old. I had brought him to the station to get a travel passport. I wanted Mom and Dad to meet him before that, but I hesitated until I felt he was old enough to understand that his grandparents were long dead, but alive in another time. My application was denied. They knew how Milo had been conceived and while it wasn't technically a crime they still used it against me to deny my son travel. That was the first time Milo had brought the pack of seeds to plant at my parent's house, so it would be a big tree when we got back to our own time. Since our travel plans had been ruined I figured I'd just pay the fine and sneak him on to the platform so he could at least see the trains up close. He was terrified of the dark tunnel and the long drop to the tracks. Or what seemed like a long drop to a five year old. He asked me what would happen if he fell on the tracks below? Would he die? I told him not to be scared. That if he ever fell, I would catch him. A stupid promise to make and one I couldn't keep. I kneel down beside the toilet and retrieve the packet of seeds.

"So you got him to change his mind to elm?" And there is an older version of myself sitting on the floor beside me, retrieving the rest of my belongings and placing everything in a neat pile on the torn paper bag. I hold up the seed packet and smile.

"Yeah, it took some time but I think what helped in my favor was that he couldn't find seeds to that death tree he was so fascinated with originally." I reply.

"Of course not, a tree that doesn't bloom doesn't have seeds does it?"

"I don't know, I'm not a botanist." Older me smiles and wraps my belongings in what remains of the paper bag.

"So what happened that day? Why did they deny his passport application?" She asks.

"You're older than me, you should remember." I reply. Older me shrugs. "I'm not sure what I know or remember. I have memories of certain things like Milo looking up that dead tree that never blooms and his grim interest in reading about it. I remember planning the trip, or trying to, and other minor things like that. Seemingly little things that I remember but they mean something bigger if I could just see the whole picture."

"Where did you come from?" I ask.

"That door." Older me nods to the entrance of the restroom and I frown. "You know what I mean." Older me nods again.

"I do know what you mean and that is where I came from. I don't remember walking into this station, or leaving home this morning. I don't even remember home this morning. The first thing that happened to me is that I was standing outside that door. And I felt like coming in, so I did and I saw you on the floor, with your spilled belongings, so I helped you pick your stuff up. Maybe you can help me with the rest." I sit on the floor with my back resting against the toilet seat.

"You're the sixth version of myself that I've met today. And one of two that's been at least a little enlightening to what's going on. I still don't understand it completely but I wonder if it's something at all like how Milo felt all his life?"

"He didn't know where he belonged, that's why he did it." Older me rests her back against the stall door. I scowl at her.

"You don't know what you're talking about. You just said yourself you don't even know why you're here." I whisper while trying to hold back tears. My son was in my hands and then a moment later he wasn't.

"I may not understand why we're both here now but I know what I'm talking about. You conceived him in a time when he shouldn't have been conceived. You gave birth to him in a time he wasn't meant for."

"If Milo wasn't meant to be born, the Creator wouldn't have let him be born." Older me shrugs.

"I'm starting to believe the flesh has its own will and so does mankind. And that will doesn't always line up with the Creator's like it should. And didn't you stop believing in God when the Consortium and the station came to be? It's the will of some to create their own purpose. Milo had no purpose at all and he grew up struggling to find it."

"His purpose was to be my son." I reply, my older self disagrees.

"A person needs more purpose than that. If his identity is built around being something to you and nothing else, what happens to him when you die and his identity dies with you? We need more. People need more or all we have is a wasted life." I look away and wipe my eyes.

"So now you know my son better than I do?" I ask.

"You mean our son. And I'm just saying it's only natural to seek out a purpose. Milo couldn't find a reason while trapped in a time that he knew he didn't belong. And he took the only way out that he could find. Everyone is born into the time they belong for a reason, born … for such a time as this, whether they agree with that decision or not. The time to do something they could do no other time or it would have no relevancy in another time. Our son was not meant to be born in that time or that way. It's why Elijah didn't love him. It's why we didn't love him."

"I did love him!" I scream. "I do love him. It's why I was going to take him to see Dad. I thought if we could go back to another time and he could meet his grandparents back when things were happy and right and spend some time with them it would … I don't know, bring him some kind of joy. Give him a reason to…"

"To want to stay." Older me finishes my thought and I shut my eyes.

"Micah didn't love him either. When Elijah left I thought possibly Micah and I could reconnect. I mean I knew he was still married and had kids of his own, but I entertained the idea that if maybe Milo could get to know his dad, he wouldn't be so sad. So depressed and hard to talk to. It was like his whole life was some kind of dark place I couldn't pull him out of. Micah's wife left him after the child support hearing. And he never missed a payment but he wanted nothing else to do with me or Milo. I had no care for anyone else. I felt no shame for what I'd done, not at the time I was doing it anyway. I spent so much time angry about the joy Micah had in his life I missed the opportunities to find it in my own. You know I saw my six-year-old self today and when I looked at her I didn't see the woman who would grow up to do the things that I've done. I didn't see hate and bitterness in her. How is that possible? How did I become this?" I pull some tissue off the roll as older me looks away not wanting to see me cry.

"That six-year old didn't know her mother was dead. She didn't know loss, hate or bitterness that comes from being robbed of something or someone. Or maybe we don't know what we are actually capable of until we do it? Outlooks change as we grow up. Environment plays a role in our lives too. Or maybe what we had the will and the heart to do was wasted in the wrong direction?" Older me explains. I had killed my son by forcing his life. By trying to create on my own, what I didn't trust someone greater than me or the world to do. Her words, "for such a time as this", hit me again. Reminded me of a Bible story my mother used to read about a queen who has to save a nation. We are born—when, where and how—for a reason. For a purpose. A purpose that could seem small or large to anyone else, but that doesn't change the fact that it is our purpose. And when we live it, fulfill it, there is a sense of accomplishment that can outdo any sensation of what we think will make us happy. Milo had no purpose, at least none for himself, and certainly not in the time he lived. His purpose for me was to make me a mother, to give me a family that had been taken from me. The family I was afraid to wait for because time seemed to go by too fast. My only thought was to satisfy myself with what I wanted at the cost of another's freedom. I had used people and hurt people. And to fight the guilt, I always had an excuse on hand. And for what, so I could be here now repeating a life that I had failed in over and over again? I felt right then, that I was the one without a purpose. The one without a reason to my life. While I was trying to control everyone else, the Consortium was now in control of me. And they weren't going to let me go. I look at my older self.

"I've been seeing myself all day and I couldn't understand why. Until now. Something the Secretary said about what the high court was doing, but it wasn't working. But if it wasn't working why am I seeing you now? You must be here for another reason?" Older me looks concerned.

"The problem is that I don't know how I got here. I don't remember time jumping through any portal or taking the train. I have no idea what I'm here for." Older me looks anxious. I stare at the door and smile bitterly. "No one has walked through that door since we've been in here. Same thing happened with my younger self when I went to see the Secretary and when I spent quite a bit of time in the station café with another younger version of myself. A station full of people and yet we were alone and uninterrupted." Older me looks at the floor.

"I'm sorry. I don't know what this is all about. I wish I knew a way to end this. I wish there was something in this world, even in this station that the Consortium couldn't control. Something that could help us end…" I look up and older me is gone. She had gone off script, really trying to help me was against what they wanted and just like that the Consortium had shown their cards. I smile to myself thinking maybe she'd done it on purpose. Just to prove something. I'm glad if she had. Glad to see that at possibly ninety years in, I hadn't lost my sense of defiance of the Consortium even at the cost of my own existence. But the Consortium didn't control my existence like I thought. There was much more to my release from the Preservation that even they didn't understand. I stand up and leave the stall. I straighten my clothing and step outside.

CHAPTER TWELVE

You may remember when I mentioned earlier that I'd only ever encountered myself once before in the station and that I wouldn't talk about that one time. Well, it would seem with all the strange things going on today that I have no other choice but to talk about that one time. It happened when I was about sixteen years old. I was at the sixth year station with Dad. He was trying to get his travel passport renewed although since Mom's death he never used it. Maybe coming to the station gave him something to do. Either way he was in the passport office filling out a mundane application when I got bored. I wandered off down some hallway and found myself right outside the infirmary. I stood in the doorway of the tiny makeshift medical room and watched a man with a bad head wound just sitting on the edge of a gurney holding gauze to his forehead. The blood had filled the white material red and was dripping down the side of his face. He seemed not to notice. There was a child sitting in the corner beside his mother who I would guess was pregnant by the way she was gripping her small belly. It was never a good idea for pregnant women to jump. Even though I had chanced it. I wondered why no one was helping anyone. Where were the nurses and doctors? I walked further into the room and found the professionals surrounding a single bed. I drew closer not knowing that what I was going to see would affect me like it did. When I laid eyes on my own dying body I inhaled sharply. I couldn't tell my age exactly, maybe late thirties, early forties? But even under all the blood I still knew it was me. My jet black hair spotted with gray strands and stuck to my skin by the sweat of my forehead as I struggled, gasping for air. My shirt was soaked in blood and my right arm looked like it was badly burned. She stared at me in panic, her eyes pleading for help and I stared back at her in complete horror. It was the first and I thought, only time I would ever encounter myself. And I was dying. In fact I stood there long enough to watch myself die. Some doctor injected me with something and called it and that was that. Her eyes open staring at another version of herself in what should've been a forgettable moment of her life while she was at the end of her own. I didn't know what to do or how to process such a thing. I backed out of the room and hurried down the hall to find Dad still in line, waiting patiently. I saw him and just cried. I cried as he held me, embarrassed and confused at the same time by the crowd of travelers staring at us. I'd only been gone a few minutes and everything had changed. I saw how short my life was and it put me in a sort of panic to do all the things I was afraid I would never experience. I didn't want to miss anything. Another strange thing about that encounter was that the version of me that died at the station was never mentioned on the news. I never told anyone what I'd seen. I never found out what happened. But after that day I became terrified of my own impending death. Of an unfinished life and no one to remember me; or at least anything good about me. It may seem selfish, but it was just how I felt at the time.

When I exit the restroom the station floor is completely empty. It's evening now. And while the station remains open until midnight, there are fewer travelers when it gets dark. I step cautiously into the hallway and search the floor. I sit on a bench by the elevators and set my torn bag down. I have five dollars left to my name. Not nearly enough for a black market passport. Milo's seed packet is still intact. I find my expired identification, a packet of gum, my dad's watch, two outdated credit cards to accounts closed upon my arrest and a single Preservation-issued ticket. Who had given me this ticket? I stare at the ceiling trying to remember the process of my release. I'm sure the Secretary is wrong and that my release papers have disappeared because the Consortium wanted them to. But as hard as I try, I can't remember a single thing about my release. Not even the bus ride to the station. I remember it because I know that's how parolees are brought to the station, but I can't actually remember being on the bus. And my time in the Preservation? I'm sure I was there. I remember my first day. That wasn't a suggestion of what could happen. It had happened. I remember being booked and the bracelet set on my wrist. I remember my first day. And only my first day. Of course I only remember my first day! I read my ticket. The issue date is for the seventieth year station on the day Milo died. This was my ticket to see my parents that day. Milo had his own ticket folded up inside the black-market passport I'd gotten for him. I must've looked insane waving this thing around like it was proof of something other than my mental imbalance. Why did I still have this ticket?

I shred the ticket and toss the remains in the garbage can beside me. Like a wave I think of the versions of myself that remember some things but not others. The crimes I committed and don't even remember. I had abused time, like everyone else. And now I'd been seeing versions of myself, possibly to guilt me from what I'd done and was going to do, whatever that was. But instead each encounter seemed to be driving me forward to that destination, that event. Each one representing a part of me that didn't mean to be a bad person but had given up on doing anything good. And my final self, what had she said? Something the Consortium couldn't control. They controlled time, life, death, freedom, the future even. But there was one thing they had no hold on. I leave the rest of my belongings on the bench, except the packet of seeds and my father's watch and I hurry to the elevators. I wasn't sure if they were coming for me yet but it didn't matter. I was made for such a time as this.

CHAPTER THIRTEEN

When I enter the first floor lobby, I'm surprised to see a few people remaining. Most likely arriving or departing for the final trips of the day. According to Dad's watch there is only an hour left until the final train departs and the station prepares to close. I needed to reach the subway platform and I had no idea why. There are four escalators leading from the lobby to the subway platform below and each one is blocked by a guard. They wouldn't run toward me, but would wait for me to come to them. Or perhaps it was a silent way of telling me they were everywhere and that I couldn't win this? Either way the guards watch me from a distance, waiting for my next move. The phantoms knew what to do as the power goes out again and I freeze in place. Murmurs of surprise echo through the lobby as people remain still and unsure of what to do. As I mentioned before, as far as I knew there had never been a power outage in the station. I inhale sharply when I feel a man's hand grab mine gently. I attempt to pull away but I can feel the material of his business suit against my arm as he begins to lead me through the dark lobby. The guards have their flashlights out but the beams of light swirl through the air chaotically like the guards don't know what to focus on. I can't see, but I know the phantoms are circling them, distracting them. The emergency lights come on just as I reach the escalators. I don't look back as I take the unmoving stairs two at a time until I reach the bottom. My knee gives out and I stumble, hitting the concrete floor, landing on my hands and knees. The main power returns when I regain my footing. I look around but my phantom guide in the suit is gone. And I'm alone on the platform staring at the collapsed tunnel where my son is buried. Piles of broken concrete, rock and half a train remain. Scattered about are signs of a work crew but no crew. Made me wonder how hard they worked to retrieve the people stuck in the train? I push the seed packet into my back pocket and approach the debris. I stand on the edge of the platform and stare down at the rocks and visible part of the tracks below. I can hear voices at the top of the escalators which have begun to move again. I prepare to jump onto the tracks but think better of it, knowing my old knees would never make it. I sit on the edge of the platform slowly and drop down carefully. There is a flashlight resting beside some other tools. I take it and make my way through the rocks and into the back end of the derailed train. There is no power inside the last car and the only light shines through the windows from the platform and the flashlight in my hands. Once in the train I see the real damage. The cracked, filthy windows, blood stains, the smell of copper and death. I make my way delicately forward as the ceiling of the car looks ready to cave in and at the far end what was left of the train car is partially crushed and partially split open against the rocks of the fallen tunnel. The guards reach the platform and I can hear them just outside the train car as I make my way toward the wreckage which cut the train in half. It is the only way further into the tunnel and with this tunnel being out of service I was less likely to get run over by an active train while doing what I was about to do. As I slide through the ripped metal of the car I feel the cold air from the tunnel against my face. I can hear the guards entering the car the same way I did. Their boots echoing across the hard, metal floor shake the already unstable car and I can feel jagged metal graze my belly and legs. I freeze and hold my breath not wanting to get tetanus but knowing I had to keep going forward. I pull myself slowly the rest of the way through the gap of the car and reach out to more fallen rock. I feel blindly, fearing sparing one of my hands to handle the flashlight as I inch my way forward. Then suddenly the space opens up and I slip forward onto the dip of the tracks running downward at an angle. My body gives in to gravity and I drop down, sliding along the tracks with tunnel debris and various broken parts of the train. I try to catch something in the dark but I cut my hands up feeling only loose rocks and sharp materials. I try to protect my head as my slide down becomes more of a tumble. I land on something hard and metallic. Large, too. I'm resting on the remains of the front half of the train, which groans under my weight. I roll to my side and feel more cold air emanating from a broken window of the fallen car. When the tunnel collapsed, the train must've split in half and while the back half got caught under the wreckage, the front half derailed completely and tipped on its side, continued sliding on the tracks dropping further into the tunnel. The front end of the cars made it a few feet before turning sideways and getting caught horizontally in the tunnel. With my added weight it wouldn't stay still for much longer. I pull myself through the window of the car and collapse on a seat slowly. I cover my nose, smelling the dead bodies that were once there. The survivors, which I'm sure were few, and the fatalities, which I'm sure were many, were rescued and cleared from the train after the crash, but it would take some time before the remains of the train itself was pulled from the tunnel and the tunnel was rebuilt and reopened for travel. It was completely dark inside, and I didn't want to use my flashlight, but I had to see where I was going. The bulb flickers to life and I stare in horror at the blood stains on the seats, the walls, the windows. Was that a severed limb? I pull the light away in a panic, not wanting to be sure of what I saw. The beam wasn't very large, and I couldn't see it clearly. I would just leave it at that. When Milo jumped off that platform I only considered his death and the mistakes I made that led to it. I hadn't even thought of these people. These people I didn't know, but I had murdered them. I didn't go after the Consortium with the intent of hurting so many innocent people, but I had caused all of this. I use my shirt to wipe the sweat from my face and continue across the car to the opposite side where I can make out more tracks leading down toward a faint light at the bottom of the tunnel. I shine my flashlight on the edge of the broken window which is partially collapsed, but I can still fit through. I swing one leg out, then the other and freeze when the box begins to move slightly. Metal grinding on metal, brick and concrete. I shine my light again to examine the tunnel. It's a long way down. I don't think I can make it before this thing gives out. But if I couldn't make it, I wouldn't be here. I shove the flashlight in the band of my pants and with both hands I let myself down slowly on the angled tracks. I can feel them just under my toes. I inhale deeply and let go so my body can slide down and sit on the tracks. I take the flashlight and shine with one hand as I descend the tracks to the bottom, almost like a ladder. The light at the bottom of the tunnel is growing brighter and a faint bit of hope tells me I just might make it. Then I hear that grinding sound again. I look back and see figures climbing through the train. There are too many of them.

"Miss, you have to come back! It's too dangerous!" A guard calls out to me as he is trying to make his way through the very same window I entered in. More people, more guards, more weight.

"You have to go back. Your weight is going to make the rest of the train fall!" I scream back and as my voice echoes, the train groans in reply. I turn and drop my flashlight and make my way blind but with two free hands as fast as I can down the tracks toward the light at the bottom. A few rocks tumble just by my head as I am trying not to lose my grip. The light at the bottom is getting brighter now, and I'm almost there just as the front half of the train begins to roll on its caught ends in the tunnel. Tossing the guards inside around like a rotisserie. Before the cars can complete a rotation the train begins to slide, each end screeching and cutting through the concrete tunnel walls. I turn on my butt and panic slide the rest of the way down, but it becomes more of a tumble again right before I land on the corner of the tracks that level out and ignore the screaming pain in my body to jump out of the way.

The front half of the train begins to free fall, cutting through the tracks, ripping up rock and metal just before it hits the tunnel corridor at the bottom where I had just fallen only moments before. Angled the way it is, the train car is too large to fit through the alcove and instead crushes against the brick frame of the opening at the bottom, followed by a cloud of dust and rocks. I cover my face and feel the tiny pellets dig into my skin.

CHAPTER FOURTEEN

When I wake, I'm back on the platform where I started. Dust and debris cloud the air as I kneel on the platform digging through fallen rock. I stop and hold my bloody, raw hands up to my face. How did I get back here? People are screaming, some closest to the tracks like I am are bleeding and crying. Some unmoving. I look behind me and people are running toward the escalators. A medical team is running toward me. I can't make out what they are saying. I point to the rocks. To my son. "Milo is under there," I tell them. But they don't listen. They try to pull me away from the fallen tunnel and I try to fight them. "Dig him out! Please dig him out!" But they won't listen to me. I feel relief wash over me as the guards appear. They will dig Milo out. They will find my son. But instead they drag me to the ground and cuff me. I'm screaming, begging them to help Milo. They don't listen, they just drag me away. Further and further from my son, buried alive. They'll take me to the hospital. I'll be arrested and sent to the Preservation where I'll be executed after my first day. I close my eyes and when I open them again I am in the crowded lobby of the first year station searching for my clock. But the clocks on the wall are moving in reverse. The second hands ticking counter clockwise. The lobby is changing and the crowds are fading. The walls change color, the seats flexing into a more comfortable design. The screens for arrivals and departures grow larger and brighter. The ticket desks multiply per country. Looks like the sixth year station. I'm on the second floor of the remodeled station, and I don't know how I got there. I'm walking toward a portal that has been left open. The night before I had changed the bulb overhead beside the shackle hook and now I was sort of regretting what I'd done. I was angry about not being able to get a passport for Milo, so I bought a virus. Sort of. A replacement bulb for the portal with a chemical inside that would destroy the time mechanism in the station. It seemed childish and a little stupid the morning after. I enter the box to take out the bulb and the attendant returns and shouts at me. I try to explain as I'm reaching for the bulb overhead and the strange liquid leaks out burning my arm. I scream and the attendant begins to drag me out of the box. He motions for the guards nearby to take hold of me. What had just burned my arm? A group of young girls approach as I try to tell the guards not to let anyone jump. They don't listen to me and the attendant checks the bulb, seeing nothing wrong and allows one of the girls to enter the box. I'm wrestled to the ground as the young woman shouts out…

"Station One-fifty!" Her friends begin to laugh as she enters the box. "See you on the other side!" The box closes and I feel something very bad is about to happen. The light in the box is blinding bright but different. The white light is not a jump but an explosion which absorbs into the time mechanism. The bulb catapulted the blast not just through the box itself but to the next station. Killing that poor girl, the attendant and anyone else within twenty feet of the box. The explosion did of course burn out the time mechanism controlling the portals in the entire station of destination rendering them useless, which was my only intention. I never meant to kill anyone. I thought the same mechanism for the portal controlled the trains, but I was wrong. I had only cut off future portal jumps to the hundred and fiftieth station, and worse still at the cost of human lives. I try to run during the chaos of the explosion, but I'm caught and shot. I'm taken to the infirmary and injected with something to finish the job. I feel it burning through my veins as I stare at my sixteen-year-old self. I close my eyes and die.

I open my eyes and I'm in the station again. The first year's station lobby searching for my clock. They are all still going in reverse. It plays like this three more times. Three more acts of destruction working backwards from my last crime to my first. Three more times I'm killed and three more times I reappear in the middle of the first year station searching for my clock and believing that I've just been paroled from the Preservation. I try to pull back, realizing I've fallen into a time loop. A replaying of the timelines I've lived and died and returned. The walls of the first year station turn to brick. The glossy tile floors turn to glass, and I can see gold gears like a clock but larger beneath my feet. I reach down to touch the gears but the glossy tile returns and when I stand up the station is gone and I'm in an office. A trailer actually. A large trailer filled with half a dozen desks, twice as many file cabinets and a few outdated computers and two women talking at a single desk while eating a pizza. "You mean you haven't thought of a name yet?" Asks the first woman. The pregnant woman next to her shrugs.

"I've thought of plenty of names but you know how he is. He wants to name her after his mother."

"Well, why not? She is your mother-in-law." The pregnant woman scowls.

"Yes, the mother-in-law who was completely against us getting married in the first place. Why would I honor her with my first child? Or any of my children, for that matter? She's lucky if I let her see them." Her coworker smiles, but it seems forced. The mother-to-be doesn't notice.

"Well, you can always use my name? Jasmine has a nice ring to it," the coworker replies.

"It's cute, but it kinda reminds me of that lamp cartoon, with the carpet." The pregnant woman continues with a look of displeasure as Jasmine looks offended. The pregnant woman notices this time.

"Fine, name her whatever you want…" Jasmine replies.

"I'm sorry, Jas, I didn't mean it like that. It's a beautiful name and I would pick that over Elsa any day."

"Yeah, right." Jasmine tosses a pizza crust playfully at her friend. "Forget you, Camille." I study the pregnant woman sharply, confused. Camille dodges the crust and is laughing as she reaches for her cup. Jasmine's smile falls as she watches Camille finish her drink. A pained look on her face. Camille does not notice as she continues talking, mostly to herself.

"I still have time. I'm sure I'll come up with something … what's wrong?" Camille notices the expression on Jasmine's face. Camille looks concerned. Jasmine realizes she is giving too much away and forces another smile.

"Nothing. I was just thinking about this job and how much it's going to suck when you take maternity. You promise you'll come back?" Camille stands up showing her growing belly.

"I promise nothing." Camille smiles. "And now I'm off to the bathroom for the hundredth time today." I watch my mother exit the office for the restroom. I know she can't see or hear me, so I don't bother reaching out to her. She looks so young. This was the office she worked in before the completion of the station. Mother was an assistant to the Station Design Committee. They spent years working on the structure of the station. How the departments would be broken up by nations and how the trains would travel through time. It would be another six and a half years before their work was completed and the first year station was open for use. Once my mother was gone, her coworker, Jasmine stands up slowly from her desk and drops the remains of her own lunch in the garbage. Seems Jasmine had lost her appetite over what she'd done. I watch her pull a plastic bag out of her pocket. She crumples the empty bag in her fist and drops it in the trash. The devastation on Jasmine's face says it all. One of those moments where a person does the worse thing they could do to another person to gain what they think they want most of all. But then you realize a little too late that it wasn't worth it and you've priced your own soul. As well as the life of another human being. Jasmine got a promotion to Lead Station Designer for each year of the station. At the cost of killing me for what should've been the last time.

When my mother returned to work two years after her 'miscarriage' with a baby daughter no one could explain, Jasmine's guilt got the better of her as did a few glasses of wine and a wet road at night. I sit on the edge of Jasmine's desk when I feel a sharp jab in my arm. "Ow, not again!" I hiss and look down and nearly fall out of a large tree. "Careful, Mom!" Milo reaches out to check my arm as we are sitting on a large wood base in the middle of the tree, which was all my dad had managed to complete of the clubhouse. A branch was digging into my right arm and another jabbing me in the back. This was getting uncomfortable as I was suddenly reminded of my age. Ten-year-old Milo is playing doctor as he checks my arm for any blood. He notices the scratch on my ankle that I got as we were climbing the tree. "You're bleeding, Mom!" I try to wipe the dried blood away and pull the hem of my pants down over the cuts. "It's okay, it's just a little scratch." I brush a leaf out of his hair as he stares out at the small community of houses nearby. "Next time you come up to my place to visit, I'll make it safer for you." His concern and adult personality makes me smile. But I won't tell him about the branch digging into my back right now. Instead I shift discreetly and try to get comfortable on the creaking slab of wood while avoiding any other part of the tree. I want to enjoy the view with my son. I'm pregnant again and this might be one of the last moments I have with just me and him for a while. The last time I can really notice him. Twins this time. Elijah was more excited than I was. When I told him I was pregnant finally, after all this time, I just looked at his face.

Studied his eyes real close like I was trying to read his mind. I felt deep down inside of myself that he would use this as a way to push Milo out. Micah and his new wife had baby number two on the way, and while Micah was a great dad, and I didn't doubt he loved his son, Milo was still stuck without a real father between two growing families. His biological dad barely had time for him anymore, and I feared his step-dad would follow. If I could redo things, I don't know what I would change. Micah and I were good when we were together, but it didn't last, and Milo suffered for it. And I love Elijah and I believe he really loves Milo. He always treated him like his own, but still, there was something there, that nagging feeling like he was keeping Milo at a distance while waiting for children of his own blood. Elijah took him to games and helped him with his homework. We did things as a family all the time, but how long could the peace last? Milo placed a figurine in my hand as he was explaining some sort of show I didn't even know he was a fan of. I nod, not really listening and I think about that one thing I was afraid of in myself. What if I treated Milo differently when the babies were born, too? What if I got overwhelmed? Or distracted? Or just tired? I didn't want to lose that bond between us. To see how he was becoming his own person. To hear about what excited him, what his goals were. Even if those goals right now were the latest video games or some cartoon I didn't understand at all. But now what would become of him? Would I still be there for him after the babies were born? Would he see them as his family? Would he still feel like one of us, even without me? Another sharp jab from the tree as I forget for a moment to sit up straight. Milo looks at me to make sure I'm still listening. I smile and he continues.

I don't want to blink. It's like a dream you immerse yourself in, and suddenly it's over and you're awake. You shut your eyes again but you can't go back. I blink anyway and feel my face pressed against the glass floor of the large room I landed in when the front half of the train hit the tunnel entrance. I'm lying on my stomach and I push myself up slowly to my hands and knees. When I open my eyes, I can see part of the time mechanism directly beneath me. Gears and cogs of solid gold all winding and twisting together like a very fancy, very large clock. I roll into a sitting position and study the room. I'm in a large, circular-shaped chamber. The walls are made of red brick with four tunnel entrances. One for each quadrant going north, south, east and west. The tracks for each quadrant head down the tunnels, into the chamber and end about five or six inches into the glass floor. The track ends are embedded in the glass somehow. Each track drops into the glass where the train is … absorbed you could say, into the time mechanism in the floor. The floor of the chamber and the mechanism itself stretch at least fifty, maybe sixty, feet across the room. The vast mechanism is continually moving. And just touching the glass over it for long enough can pull someone into a time loop. Unlike the trains, when I fell on the mechanism after the crash, my jump was uncontrolled by me. But purposeful in showing me what did happen in many timelines and what could've happened in another had time travel not changed things. My mother's friend had put something in her drink and caused her to miscarry when she was pregnant with me. This was the Consortium's last attempt on my life and the very attempt that caused my existence and their destruction.

Cathy Morgan never existed. Maybe there was a woman by that name, somewhere in the world and somewhere in time, but I never met her. And she was no relation to me. She was merely a name to explain to the public why the phantoms existed. And why a young woman, then a woman, then an older woman, then an old woman kept appearing in the center of the first year station lobby, staring at a clock and claiming she was going home. The staff was used to me by now. While not every passenger had encountered me, I had become a sort of fixture. A phantom no one could place or understand. One of "Geenie's" children that had more depth than the others. Closer to existing than she should. It's what people assumed because no one ever tried to find the phantom of "Geenie" herself.

When the time travel station was completed someone went forward in time. As far as they could go. I have no idea who they were or how they got the honor of such a first trip, but whatever happened they saw something they didn't like. They saw an old woman desperate to undo it all by destroying the station. She failed in many of her attempts but succeeded in planting a seed of fear. The Consortium couldn't allow another timeline to be created where I accomplished what I set out to do. So they planned to kill me before I could do it. Working backward from Milo's death, which they considered my final attempt at destruction. But my death didn't stop the event like they thought it would. So they went back further and tried again and again and again. Six times, leading all the way back to before I was born. After my mother's "miscarriage" the time fracture was discovered and the phantoms appeared. My children, grandchildren and great grand-children roaming in and out existence wreaking havoc they had inherited from me. So Cathy Morgan was invented along with her sister "Geenie". Two women no one had ever met in person but knew all about through media lies. My mother and father never knew that their descendants were the phantoms because even though my mother had miscarried, she didn't know it, as her pregnancy continued like normal and she gave birth to a live baby girl— one that was not supposed to exist. By then my mother and father had decided on a middle ground for my name. Mom thought it would be funny to call me something Else. The Consortium couldn't understand how I was still alive and wouldn't show their cards by giving anything away of what they'd done. So I was monitored very, very closely. As my life moved forward like any normal person, my deaths which were once in reverse, followed in the forward direction. Except this time beginning at the age of nineteen, when I was first arrested in a normal timeline. After my first day at the Preservation I was executed and the next day I reappeared in the center of the first year station, still alive, still nineteen and believing I'd been released after a day. The Consortium was floored. And couldn't admit that they had killed me, so they let me go home. Dad was happy to have me back. I was killed one way or another four more times. Each time I was either arrested then executed or executed on the spot, and each time I returned to the center of the first year station thinking I'd just been paroled and with new memories of what should've happened in my timeline. Except this time the Consortium was getting fed up with me, and it was obvious that I had become a bigger nuisance than the average phantom, that one thing they couldn't control. When I returned this time they attempted to reform me in a way by guilting me with my past selves. Showing me all that I had ruined only drove me harder, sort of. There was no undoing the mistakes I made unless I undid this perversity of time itself. And this time my children were helping me. I'm sure they had something to do with Robin Green's capture, knowing he would escape and give me time to move forward. Then there was the key to the portal and so much else. They were tired of being on the brink, and so was I.

CHAPTER FIFTEEN

One tunnel was blocked by the twisted metal of the fallen train cars. The other three were still open and accessible. Why hadn't the guards come in? How long had I been in the time loop? I pull my father's watch out of my pocket and see it is broken. Now what? I kneel down and knock on the glass. It's thick and even if I managed to find something to break it, what then? Fall into a bottomless pit of golden cogs and unrestrained time. I search through the gears and cogs of the time mechanism, trying to see the bottom, trying to see some weak link in the machine. I can't even understand how it all works. I hold the seeds in my hand and press my thumb against Milo's print in blood. And like that it comes to me. Not an idea, but the train. A train is coming down the east tunnel. Its bright head lights shining directly on me. I cross the glass floor and press myself against the wall, feeling the vibration of the coming train through my entire body. As the train hits the glass, it dissolves into the glass along with the end of the tracks. But not before I watch the glass floor ripple like water. The trains open the floor. The East line completely disappears, and I kneel down hesitantly to touch the floor which has gone solid again. But as I look close into the floor I can see a faint outline of the train rounding the machinery of the mechanism in a coil shape like a snake, before it disappears completely into the golden abyss. I press my hand against the cold, smooth glass and try to think. The trains open the floor which is a part of the mechanism. As I study the floor there is a not so subtle sound behind me. I turn and look to find a single cab door from the collapsed train being ripped off the hinges of the crushed train. The metal door falls to the floor and begins to sink into the glass. Alarmed I hurry to it and catch the handle just before it can sink further into the "puddle." I maneuver the door slowly in my arms as I try to balance the weight of it in my grip. The train opens the floor … perhaps parts of the train can open the floor, too. I hold the door up like a shield and stare into the depths of the floor. Can I really do this? I look at the seed packet in my hands.

"If you fall, I'll catch you." I breathe deeply, shut my eyes and tip forward, resting all my weight on the door, expecting to hit solid floor but refusing to open my eyes when my body keeps going. I feel a rush of cold and a tingling all over my skin.

When I wake I'm at the bottom of a golden room. Actually it wasn't so much the room that was golden as the gears overhead and around me reflecting off the walls and the floor, making it seem golden. I hear voices. Many people talking all at once in different languages, accents. I can hear crying. Many people crying. Calling out to someone, calling out for help. Pleading for something. Seems I wasn't the only one who'd made things worse by trying to control the timing of my life. Then I see them, shadows of people spread out all across the room, within the walls, the gears of the machine, the floor even, which is some strange form and body of water rolling over my shoes and up to my ankles but my feet aren't wet. The shadows look like phantoms, changing and shifting. Growing, aging right in front of my eyes. A few of the shadows are versions of myself playing out in front of me like a film that only jumps to the important parts. This must be the very bottom of the machine. The very root of it all. The root … I open the seed packet and dump the pellets into the water like floor. They sink under the surface slowly and begin to float around my sneakers, bouncing off the tips of my shoes. Time has no balance here; it exists in a chaotic, unrestrained form. The seeds shake and split open. Tiny green vines pour out of the casings, stretching through the liquid and rising up off the floor. I stand back and the roots swell and extend upward and out forming tiny leaves and stalks. The Consortium had found a way to wield time and instead proved that humans have no understanding or control of it. Each seed has become an individual elm, the trunk of each growing larger than any tree I've ever seen. The tops of the trees begin to reach the mechanism overhead, and I look up awestruck at how quickly the trees have grown. Their massive branches unlike any other tree as they begin to press into the cogs and motors and interrupt the rotation. Some of the branches give in to the force of the machine and break, and I fear maybe it's not strong enough until I notice some of the other branches are holding. A gear is forced out of alignment with the rest of the machine and falls straight down out of the air. I brace myself for the sound of the impact on the floor but when the gear hits the bottom it is no longer gold, but worn and rusted. So old it breaks into tiny fragments that seem to turn to dust before landing in the water. I watch in amazement as other parts of the machine begin to fall corroded and rusted. What is made by man lasts only for a time. It is not eternal. The trees ascend higher and higher into the machine. Their roots growing so thick and fast they carpet the floor, digging into the floor even. I can make out tiny cracks in the tile as the roots force their way even deeper, searching for more moisture maybe? As the floor begins to shift, I see the walls around me following. A large crack forms in one wall at the base and continuing straight up until I can't see it anymore. The entire room is coming undone. I stand on the largest root nearest me as the floor crumbles and falls away. Crawling on hands and knees I scale the root until I reach the massive trunk. This tree has gotten so large I can't even see around it. I place my hand against the trunk and look up. As the mechanism is crumbling I am shielded from the falling pieces under the various branches and vibrant leaves. The golden gears continue to stall and are dislodged with such force some of them project straight up hitting the underside of the glass floor then back down again, crashing into other parts of the mechanism. Branches break free and reach above the machine even. As the mechanism is being forced apart, even the brick walls of the upper level begin to crack under the strength of the roots. The body of the room gives way and bricks tumble down into the abyss near me. As I watch the destruction I entertain the idea that all this is for nothing. What if I succeed, just to have someone else, in another age, another place, discover a way to rebuild it all? The remains of the crushed train are shaken loose from the entrance of the tunnel and tumble straight into the mechanism. And I think to myself, let them rebuild, and when they do there will be someone just like me to tear it all down again. As the train car passes the mechanism I can just make it out through the thick trees. The train focuses in and out like a phantom as it falls, and just as it is about to reach the floor only a few feet from me I feel everything come to a stop. I hold tight to the trunk and shut my eyes as my whole world comes to an end. And I've never been so happy.

CHAPTER SIXTEEN

"Happy birthday to … wait a minute, wait a minute. See, you're coming in too high. It's happy birthday to you. Go higher on the 'you.'" My father is explaining to my husband Elijah how to properly sing happy birthday to me, even though the song and the cake were almost an hour ago. I can see them from my spot on the kid's swing set in the backyard as they replay the song from the kitchen. Dad isn't drunk. He's just eccentric. More so at his age. I was comfortable watching from the swing as Mom intervenes to save poor Elijah.

"Okay mister, that's enough singing for today. How about you help me finish this word game with the kids?" Mom leads Dad out of the kitchen, and I watch Elijah as he is finally alone. He is staring at something out of view beneath the window. Something on the kitchen table, possibly the remains of my birthday cake. He places his hands over his eyes and rubs his weary face. He's still so handsome to me. Especially after all these years together. I watch Elijah set something in the sink and exit the kitchen. He enters the living room and forces a smile with the kids as they are all sitting around the dining room table in teams over the game board.

"Mom?" Milo approaches me from the garage with a frown as he pulls his coat off.

"What's wrong?" I ask.

"It's so cold out here. You're not cold?" He asks while pulling his coat over me before I can answer. Actually I hadn't felt the cold really until he said something. Lost in my thoughts, I guess. Milo sits in the swing beside me, and we're both careful not to swing too hard, knowing this is a set made for children and two adults can pulls the structure right up out of the ground.

"Not a word game fan?" I ask Milo. He raises an eyebrow.

"Not when Grandma is playing. She can make a triple score out of "cat" and somehow get a hundred points." I throw my head back in laughter. It's true. My mother was not to be messed with when it came to words.

"Maybe we can start a sort of scavenger hunt? That might be more our speed. Of course, we probably wouldn't finish until next summer, but…"

"No, that's okay. You mind if I sit out here with you?" He asks cautiously.

"Of course I mind! Out of all my kids you're the one I really can't stand." Milo smiles even when deep down he doesn't really want to. I can see the fear on his face. He knows I'm being funny to cover my own anxiety.

"Uncle Micah called. He told me to tell you happy birthday."

"That was nice of him. Well-wishings from a distance. But you know you don't have to call him uncle. He's not really your uncle. Just your dad's friend."

"And your ex-boyfriend."

"I hate when you bring that up. I never should've told you how your dad and I met."

"I'm just saying that was pretty rough dating a guy for two years and then leaving him for his best friend, who you marry after six months."

"First off, that's not exactly how it happened. And Micah left me, sort of. And anyway we weren't meant for each other. He understood that, which is why he is happily married now…"

"For the third time." Milo interjects. I pick up a pebble from beneath my foot and toss it at him playfully.

"He's trying. Everybody struggles with what they're looking for sometimes. Micah and I were looking, just not for each other."

"You know when I was younger, whenever dad would make me mad about something I would imagine what it would be like if Uncle Micah was my dad instead."

"Oh goodness. If only you knew Micah back then. What did you imagine from him anyway?" Milo shrugs.

"Nothing really different at first. I just thought maybe he would be a cool dad that would let me do whatever I wanted. But for some reason I couldn't imagine you two together, so in my mind Micah was my dad and you were my mom but you weren't together and it made me kinda sad."

"Sad that your brother and sisters didn't exist?"

"Partly. But there was more to it. It was just so different. More complicated and after a while I just stopped doing it. Dreaming about a different life, you know." Milo was twenty years old and the eldest of my five children. My miracle baby after almost a decade of trying. Then another ten year gap between him and my twin daughters Sarah and Savannah. I used to think the age gap would bother him but really it just made it easier for him to go around telling everyone his sisters were his. "My babies," as he referred to them. He was like a little father in the making back then and he hadn't even hit his teens yet.

"Now I feel kind of guilty about it. Like I'm not thankful for the life I have. For you and dad and Sarah and Savannah, for Nathan and Geenie. I love you guys. And I'm glad my life wasn't … so empty I guess."

"You sound like a man who thinks he's about to lose everything. You're not Job, you know." Milo stares at me as he holds back tears. He says nothing, but I know what he wants to say.

"I'm still here." I take his hand in mine and we continue to swing slowly in silence.

"Mom, I'm scared. How can you not be scared? It's your body! It's not even my body and I'm terrified. And I feel guilty."

"Of what?" I ask with all concern.

"What if … I don't know how to say it. It sounds so stupid, but … what if you're sick now because I didn't appreciate you and Dad when I had the chance." I turn Milo's face to my own and we are eye-to-eye.

"You were a teenager, dreaming like a teenager does. Like some adults do. I never once doubted the love you have and I think your dad would feel the same. And I don't believe that God works that way. Of course we should be grateful for every day. Even for being born, where we are, with the talents we're given and the goals on our life. I'm grateful for you and your sisters and your brother. And you have no idea how grateful I am that you are not Micah's son." We both laugh tearfully.

"But to answer your question. I am afraid. Part of me anyway. When I was younger than you are now, I was terrified of death. I was terrified of everything I'd miss. The experiences, the relationships, everything I thought life was made up of. I thought that if I knew what was coming and when, then I could make better decisions. But living like that makes everything in a hurry. And when you're rushing you tend not to think clearly. You give up waiting on God to answer your prayers so you try to answer them for yourself. Like Abraham and Sarah. I was afraid that I would never find a career so I bounced around from job to job when it didn't work out in the first few weeks. I was afraid that I would never fall in love so I stayed with Micah longer than I should have. I was afraid I would never be a mom. Your dad and I tried for so long. I mean I was nearly forty when you were born and everyone kept trying to tell me of all the medical problems and disabilities you might have because I "waited" so long. I let them speak bad things over you and it got into my mind, my heart and it scared me how you would develop. Then you were born so … so perfect to me, the complete opposite of what was said about you, and I realized that I don't have to accept other people's logic or studies about me or my children. I didn't have to fear age or time. I didn't have to be afraid that things would never happen for me. That I would die never accomplishing anything. Even in going to heaven. And you know, to be honest, I didn't want to disappoint God by wasting my time here. Especially after He's given me so much. And it took a few decades but I finally realized that I don't need to know what's going to happen tomorrow. I'm made for right now. And I can trust God for the rest." I take my thumb and wipe Milo's tears and he stares at the fading mark circling my wrist.

"What happened to your wrist? What is that?" I stare at the mark, noticing it for the first time.

"You know I have no idea where that came from. It might have come from your grandpa's old watch that I was playing with the other day." Milo tries to fight a smile but he can't help it.

"Mom, you are so strange."

"I am, aren't I?"

"What are you two doing out here?! You're missing my vocabulary reign of terror!" My mother is calling to us from the back patio doorway. Milo and I make eye contact. Milo makes a face as we stand up from the swings and cross the backyard.

"I'm almost positive the words she uses are made up." Milo whispers to me.

"You should challenge her." I whisper back. Mom watches us with a daring gleam in her eye. Milo frowns.

"Not worth it. Let her have her win."

"Milo, you're on my team!" Mom grabs Milo and pulls him into the house as I stop just outside the sliding glass door and stare at the growing elm tree in the backyard. I look up to see the stars positioned in a glittering outline forming a shape of shiny cogs and gears in the sky.

"Thank You for another chance. I hope I made You proud."

"Mom, be on my team!" Geenie calls to me and I reenter the house and shut the door on the night.

ABOUT THE AUTHOR

Dawn Evans was born and raised in Southern California. Although she grew up a book nerd, she was never one for the classroom but spent her days until graduation in the library searching for her next read, or in her room indulging in her latest literary find. While reading always seemed to be her passion, her love for writing her own stories followed close behind. From creating fairy tales and silly soap operas for her family to writing fake advertisements, promoting ice cream over frozen yogurt as an English assignment, if she could make someone laugh with it, then she would.

While she was known for carrying a Bible in her arms as a child before she even knew how to read, it wasn't until her late twenties that Dawn found her way into a church to hear the Word of God and understand His love and intentions for her for the very first time. And years later she would begin to dive into her calling of writing about the excellence of God and the good things in life that are sometimes hard to see.

In her journey through the Word and discipleship, Dawn found a passion for writing about different walks of life and how no matter the depth of the struggle, the Lord can and will meet us there and lift us into a better place if we call on Him.

Her focus is on encouraging others in different seasons of life to look to the only real truth we have in this world and come to understand the identity of our Creator God and the heart He has for us which can only be found in the greatest book ever written.

Tomorrow Can Worry About Itself